ONE LAST GOOD TIME

ONE LAST GOOD TIME

STORIES

MICHAEL KARDOS

Press 53
Winston-Salem

Press 53, LLC
PO Box 30314
Winston-Salem, NC 27130

First Edition

Cover photo Copyright © 2011 by Megan Snider

Cover design by Kevin Morgan Watson

Author photo by Catherine Pierce

Library of Congress Control Number: 2010919570

Printed on acid-free paper
ISBN 978-1-935708-10-0

for Katie

CONTENTS

Grateful acknowledgment is made to the publications where these stories first appeared:

"Lures of Last Resort," *Crazyhorse*

"Mr. Barotta's Ashes Have the Personality of a Grouchy Old Man,"
    PRISM international

"One Last Good Time," *Gulf Coast*

"Behind the Music," *The Florida Review*

"We the People," *River City*

"Population 204," *Blackbird*

"Maximum Security," *The Southern Review*

"Two Truths and a Lie," *PRISM international*

"What's Left of Musical Giants," *PRISM international*

LURES OF LAST RESORT

O ne July morning, three men came walking up to my dad and me while we fished off the public pier. This was back in my hometown, in Breakneck Beach, home of the Breakneck Beach Sea Devils and Rex's Italian Sausages. The particular rod I was fishing with, and the reel, too, I'd gotten that spring for doing nothing more than turning a year older. I had just dropped my line into the water when I saw the three men coming our way. They weren't fishermen. Their work pants were ironed smooth, and as they got close I could smell aftershave. Their faces didn't have the wrinkles you get from squinting into the sun. Didn't carry fishing rods either, these men. One of them held an expensive-looking camera. Another carried a small plastic box. The third man didn't carry anything; he just smiled dumbly.

"Take a look at this, gentlemen," the man carrying the box said to us. His voice sounded deep and resonant like the disc jockeys that my folks listened to on the radio. *Fat Billy spinning the oldies. Big Joey bringin' it to you.* This man wasn't big, though, just tall. And skinny like me. He unclasped the box. "You gentlemen won't believe what you see."

I wasn't any gentleman. What ten-year-old is? And the green plastic box, and those feathery lures that looked like

1

little peacocks—I'd seen them before. They were Reel Catch lures, manufactured right here in Breakneck Beach, and my dad used to sell them. Until a month earlier, Dad had sold all sorts of Reel Catch gear to tackle shops and sporting-goods stores. He had spent his days driving up and down the Jersey Shore drumming up orders for reels and fillet knives and those portable toilets for boats with no johns. And lures, too, same as these.

"You'll catch your supper in no time flat," the man said. His V-neck shirt said Reel Catch in one corner and had a stitched-on logo that looked like the lures in the box.

Since mid-June we'd been fishing that pier, my dad and I, every sticky morning from sunrise to ten a.m. I'd wake to the sound of my bedroom door squeaking open. "Up and at 'em," my dad would say, then leave me in the dark to pull on some clothes while he went to the kitchen for coffee, which always smelled good even though, like beer, it was off-limits.

That summer you could have caught fish just by asking nicely. Flukes and snappers. Flounders. Bluefish. Didn't matter to me what we caught; I didn't eat fish, and Dad was allergic. (Mom would eat anything we put on her plate and pretend to like it.) At the end of the fishing pier, my dad would fillet our day's catch and separate the fillets into baggies, and when we came home we'd strut around the apartment complex like a couple of heroes, ringing doorbells and giving everybody free fish that'd stink up their apartments in about a minute. What we didn't give away my dad would put in the freezer, till the freezer had nothing but fish in it and my mother would say things like "We have enough fish, don't we?" or "Maybe tomorrow you two ought to take a rest." But we never did.

The man holding the box said, "These lures're made special like that, colorful, to attract—"

"I know exactly what they're meant to do," my dad said.

"Who the hell do you think I am? Son, why don't you tell these men who I am."

So I told them. "My dad is Lee Gernipoethy."

The men looked at one another and then back at my dad. "Well, Jesus, we didn't...we were sent out here on a little promotional stint. That's all. Giving away some lures. We didn't know..."

You say our last name like Gunnipuddy, and it's a name people don't forget. Especially when you're a big man like my dad, six-two and broad like the linebacker he'd been till senior year, when he quit high school for reasons that, though he never said so outright, had a lot to do with my being born. These men obviously had started working for Reel Catch after my dad got fired, because they hadn't recognized him. Though by now the name Gernipoethy must have already been legend. Dad had been chewed out for some minor infraction, the story goes, when he lifted his manager's desk right up in the air—and this wasn't some small desk, either—and threw it through the window. It fell two stories to the parking lot below. Then Dad spent the night in jail.

It's a story I learned years later, when I was fifteen. By then my mother had already been remarried a while. To Rodney. One night, Rodney got home from his job as customer service manager at the water company and found me in the parking lot setting free a daddy-longleg I'd caught in the bathroom sink. I'd scooped it up in my cupped hands and run outside with it tickling my palms. After I let it go, Rodney and I went inside, and Rodney got a bottle of Budweiser from the refrigerator and then told me the story of my dad's night in jail. Rodney liked to tell stories, and I didn't like the way he told this one—his eyes gleaming, hands in motion, voice animated, pausing every so often to take long swallows from his beer. It was exactly the way he told my mom and me the outrageous and sad excuses customers had for not paying their water bill. *But that's Lee*, he concluded. *That's old Lee for you. A real character, that one.*

Except he wasn't a character—he was my dad, even if I hadn't seen him in a few years—and I sat there at the kitchen table wondering what Rodney's point was in telling me a story that made my dad look foolish, till Rodney slapped me on the shoulder and said, as if we were old chums, *But you know something? You don't have one bit of your old man's mean streak in you.*

He went to the refrigerator again, I remember, and came back with two more bottles of Budweiser. *I'm going to give you a beer tonight, son*, he said, and I punched that man in the eye as hard as I could. In thirty minutes a brown shopping bag full of my clothes sat next to me on the curb where you wait for Greyhound busses to take you away to new places. Mom was still out, working the four-to-midnight shift at the Breakneck Beach Diner, and I knew she'd be heartbroken. But I went anyway. When you make up your mind to move on, you move on. And so that's what I did.

Back when I was ten, though, I didn't know the details of Dad's job or how he lost it. I knew that suddenly he had time for fishing, and that he expected me to come along. But once our lines were in the water, he had this way of forgetting I was even there, of looking off at the horizon for long periods, not answering my questions about why clouds went pink at sunrise, or whether fish felt pain when they bit the hook, or whether a tidal wave would demolish this whole town. *Dad?* I would say, trying to draw him back to me. Nothing. *Dad!* My dad was obviously involved in some heavy thinking. All the same, I'd have preferred that he answer my questions.

"Give my son some lures, then, if that's what you're here to do." Dad sure was paying attention now, watching the men hard. The man holding the box of lures handed me three of them. "Is that all you're planning to give my kid? Kid's a good fisherman, needs plenty of lures."

"It's okay, Dad," I said. "Three's enough." But my dad wasn't listening. He had taken a small step closer to the man with the lures, and the men were glancing down at the fishing knife that hung free in Dad's belt. They were taking that knife seriously. Dad spat off to the side, looked again at the man holding the lures, and raised his eyebrows as if waiting for an answer.

The man handed me the entire box. Must've been thirty lures in there, all peacock-looking and ready for action.

"Thanks," I said, taking the box.

"No thanks necessary, son," my dad said. "That's his job, giving out fishing tackle. Don't know what that other man's job is"—he nodded to the dumb-looking one—"I never heard of it taking two men to hand out lures. Big waste of money, you ask me."

"We're on the same sales team," the man said, the man who barely reached my dad's chin.

"Sales team!" My dad ran a hand through his hair. "Fellows are teammates? Like in baseball?" He shook his head in disbelief. "Salesmen have what're called territories," he explained to me. "If they start working in pairs, then they've got to start splitting commissions." He waited for them to dispute what he'd said, but they didn't. "And *that* man"—he nodded to the photographer—"it's that man's job to take pictures of the people who've gotten the lures. Action photos, preferably. Isn't that right? For next year's catalogue?"

The photographer said, "Or the local paper. Or both."

"Well, then," my dad said to me, "let's catch some fish." He pulled the knife from his belt, cut off the lure he'd been using, and dropped it into the little bucket where we kept our tackle. Then he removed one of the Reel Catch lures from its plastic package and tied it on. He did the same with my line, too, then tucked the knife back through his belt. This all took a few minutes. Some other fishermen were on the pier that morning, but I had all the giveaways. So the three men waited.

The fishing pier wasn't two blocks from the firehouse, and as Dad was slowly tying on the Reel Catch lures—deliberately slowly, I'm sure, because I'd seen him tie on lures before in two seconds—the firehouse started blaring its siren. Loudest thing you ever heard. Happened almost every day, far more often than there could be fires. I yelled from deep within my throat: "I love you Carla Van Sickle I love you Carla Van Sickle I love you Carla Van Sickle!" Over and over I yelled it, for maybe thirty seconds. What I knew was, as long as you matched your yelling to the pitch of the siren, nobody could hear you. It could be your own secret. Carla was the third-smartest and second-prettiest girl in my class, and I loved her with a wholeness that I had never loved anybody with before or probably ever would again. She was skinny, with eyes the color of a first-place ribbon and a voice like smooth paint. She wore cutoffs that her mom trimmed for her, and little white strands of denim were always draping down her legs. I walked into walls for her, literally missed doors on purpose, because when I did, she laughed, and her laugh was worth an army of bruises.

By the time the siren died down again, Dad had the Reel Catch lures on. I set down the plastic box at my feet and we both cast our lines into the water. Fluke, we were going for, so we stood there jiggling our rods, waiting for the fish to bite.

"Get yourself ready," Dad said to the photographer.

"Are we going to be in the newspaper?" I asked my dad, and the end of my rod bent over. I yanked the rod upward, and the reel made a metallic buzzing sound, an exhilarating sound, the sound of a big fish. Everything that had been said or thought only seconds before was now miles in the past.

"Dad!" My rod bent like crazy. "I got one!"

The three men came closer. The photographer raised

his camera. I imagined Dad and me in the paper, the sports section, and we were smiling big newsprint teeth, and there was a caption that made us seem tough and outdoorsy. I could smell fish blood.

But my dad shook his head. "Nah—he's only caught the ground. Look." He took the rod from my hands and held it steady. The whirring stopped and the rod straightened. He yanked the rod again—more whirring. "See? It's just the ground."

The men exhaled. The photographer lowered his camera.

My dad pulled the knife from his belt and cut the line. "That's one Reel Catch lure we won't be seeing again."

Once the Reel Catch reps saw we weren't catching any fish with their tackle, they and the photographer started muttering to one another about having to get back to the showroom. Yet they waited, and at first Dad appeared to pay no notice, just kept jerking his fishing rod up and down. Finally, without turning toward them, he said, "I don't think you men are going to get what you're after today." Without another word, the men nodded and slunk away.

As soon as they were gone, Dad reeled in his line. "There's a reason I don't use these lures, son. See that hook?" He laid the Reel Catch lure on his palm. "Hook's too big for that lure. The design's all wrong."

I reeled in my line, and we rigged up our old lures again. Dad put the Reel Catch lures back into the plastic box and closed the clasp. "Those are lures of last resort," he said. "If I was stranded on a deserted island with no food, I'd rather try clubbing fish over the head than catching them with a Reel Catch lure."

I laughed, and cast my line into the water. Dad told me that it's more important for lures to reflect light off the sun than it is for them to look like actual fish. Better off using tin foil than some fancy colorful lure.

"I'd rather jump into the water and grab them myself," I said, "than catch them with a Reel Catch lure."

My dad cast his own line into the water. "I'd rather call them on the phone, invite them to dinner, than catch them with a Reel Catch lure."

"I'd rather shoot them with a gun," I said, looking up at my dad, "than catch them with a Reel Catch lure."

"Guns are dangerous," my dad said. "You keep away from guns."

We stood there for a while, not talking, just fishing, until my dad spat over the end of the pier, sized me up, and said, "Biggest animal on Earth's the blue whale, not some dinosaur." Then he said, "Whales eat a lot of plankton. Tons and tons of it."

My dad had been doing some heavy thinking on the pier, but now he was done with thinking. Now he was looking at me, telling me that love made you do crazy things, but that sometimes crazy things were called for. Saying that I'm likely to grow to his height if I eat and sleep enough. That the tide rises just over six feet during a full moon. He was answering every question I'd ever asked, and others I'd forgotten or never asked in the first place.

He said that fighting never got you anywhere, and that only lazy people fished past noon. That tidal waves didn't ever hit this coast. But yes, in theory the town would flood.

He didn't speak quickly, yet there was urgency in his voice as if what he was telling me was vitally important. I know now he believed he was talking with me, father to son, for the last time, and so he was making up for all the lost moments, and the lost moments to come. I have no idea what he had planned, specifically, beyond getting in his car and driving in some predetermined direction, but my hunch is that his destination was beside the point. After leaving Breakneck Beach myself at fifteen, I picked up and moved every year or two, and not once did the destination matter at all. It's more a feeling that if you stay, your bones will crush. Your gut will bleed. You'll behave in a way you can't live with.

A dull knife is more dangerous than a sharp one, he said. In lake fishing, you're better off along the shoreline than in the middle of the lake. He said that every mass has gravity— it's why the Earth revolves around the sun, and why the moon revolves around the Earth. An albacore fights like a fish twice its size. "Albacore's the best thing you'll ever catch," he said, and I imagined what a battle that must be.

"Do you know why the beach erodes?" my dad asked.

I said that I didn't.

So he told me. And then he told me some more.

The next morning at eight-thirty, I got out of bed and found Mom at the kitchen table staring at the wall, a half-eaten English muffin on her plate. The radio was on, the volume low, probably so that it wouldn't wake me. I was almost next to her before she seemed to notice me.

"Where's Dad?" I asked.

Mom pursed her lips, stood, and went to the refrigerator. "Which jelly do you want?" She opened the refrigerator door. "Strawberry?"

"Where is he?" I sat down in one of the kitchen chairs. But she didn't answer me. She'd begun moving things around in the refrigerator, slamming down jars on the shelves, rearranging everything. I started to feel seasick. "Mom?" I tried to sound calm, although I could feel my neck beating and the spit in my mouth going dry. "What's going on? Where is he?"

"*Where is he, where is he...*" She slammed the refrigerator door and spun to glare at me. I must have shrunk away, because then her face softened and she came over to the table. She stood over me for a few seconds, just looking.

"Listen to me. Just be quiet and listen." She sat next to me at the table. Mom still had long hair then, and some strands had fallen over her face, but she didn't seem to notice. She was watching me closely. "You're ten years old and I'm not going to lie to you. You think your father's a great man, don't you? Your hero, probably. He isn't perfect, you know." She picked up her English muffin, examined it, and put it back in her plate.

I asked her for the millionth time, Where *was* he?

"How the hell should I know?" Mom scrunched up her face like she might sneeze, but she didn't. She stayed frozen that way while the clock over the stove clicked a few times. Then she said, "Sorry. Okay? I'm sorry. I'm just telling you how it is. He leaves sometimes, but he always comes home. The last time, you were too young for me to explain what was going on. You probably don't even remember."

But suddenly I did remember. Sort of. Actually, all I remembered was the seasick feeling, as if the apartment building were rolling in waves, same as I was feeling now. "How many times has he left?" I asked.

"Several times," she said. "But not for a few years."

"Where does he go?"

"That depends. It all depends."

"Why does he leave?" I asked. We were both calming down, now. We were just talking. I was asking questions, and my mother was answering them.

"Your father would say for love. He loves me, so he leaves. He loves me, so he returns. Love, love, love. So finally I said to him…" She shook her head. "Well, never mind what I said to him. But don't worry. He'll be back. I'm not going to lie to you. Your father's left, but he's coming back. He'll be back."

Either Dad's departures had lost their weight, or else Mom needed to act as if they had, because she spent the day doing ordinary things. Sweeping. Studying for a class she was taking in stenography. Humming along to the radio. Making me snacks: a plate of bologna and cheese, crackers, slices of carrots.

I couldn't eat. For two days I sat on the rug in the living room with one hand on the telephone, convincing myself that I could feel it preparing to ring. Convinced that if one hand *weren't* on the phone, then it wouldn't ring and it would be my fault.

"Go outside," my mother told me. "I'll let you know if anybody calls."

On the third day, I woke up early without even meaning to, before sunup, and decided to be a man. I got my fishing rod and tackle from behind the washing machine, and without waking Mom I went outside and walked the five blocks to the fishing pier. I didn't want to use the regular lures. They were my dad's, and I didn't want any help from him or his lures. And so I rigged up one of my own—the Reel Catch lures—but all morning long I didn't get a single hit. Dad had been right about one thing: these lures were no good.

A few of the usual fishermen were out, all grown men, everyone standing at a polite distance from one another and looking off to the horizon. Closest to me, a thin, silver-haired man wearing overalls and dirty sneakers uncapped a thermos and poured himself a steaming drink into the lid. He met my gaze while taking a sip and then saluted me with the lid. We were just two men, fishing. I laid down my rod and went over to him.

"Is that coffee?"

When he said that it was, I asked him for a sip. The man creased his forehead at me, he tilted his head, but then he offered the thermos lid and said to be careful, it's hot. I hadn't ever drunk coffee before, and it tasted as bitter as I imagined tar must, but I swallowed a big mouthful anyway, burning my throat some, said thank you, and went for my rod again.

The morning was cooler than usual, the ocean calm, and watching the horizon myself I started making plans. I would quit school and find a job earning money for Mom and me. I imagined starting my own newspaper where I would sell advertising space to companies like Reel Catch. I was ten, but I swear I thought of that idea and several others as well. I would become famous for having a successful newspaper and being so young. I decided to start my newspaper that afternoon, walking door-to-door in the apartment building and selling subscriptions.

When I got home, drunk from my own ideas, both my parents were sitting at the kitchen table, their pinkies interlocked. Mom's eyes were red, but she was smiling and seemed content. Proud almost, as if she'd won a bet with herself. Dad's hair was mussed, he was unshaven, but other than that it could have been any other summer morning.

"Son," my dad said, and nodded as if we were both men who understood something important.

But I understood nothing. Seeing him, all I knew was that I wouldn't get to prove myself after all. There would be no newspaper, no fame, because my dad had failed at something as easy as walking out on us. And feeling disappointed in him made me feel shameful for feeling disappointed, and that, you can imagine, led me to feeling angry, furious, for having been made to feel shame over how I was feeling, which isn't exactly something that a person had any control over. Not at ten. Not when we're talking about a person's dad leaving and then coming home again. I glared at him.

"Well?" he said, his eyes clear and wide and inviting. "Were they biting?"

For a moment I'd forgotten I was carrying a fishing rod. "Like crazy," I said, and went to put away the gear and pretend that he had never even come home. I made it as far as the doorway when my dad must have decided it wasn't time yet to be written off by his own damn son.

"What kind of fish did you catch?"

"Bluefish," I said. "Big ones. And an albacore." I turned around to face him. He was sitting back in his chair, his arms folded, his gaze on me. "Yeah, I did. And you were right about albacore, it really…"—and then I realized too late that he had drawn me into the lie so that he could catch me in it and watch me thrash around.

MR. BAROTTA'S ASHES
HAVE THE PERSONALITY
OF A GROUCHY OLD MAN

The baby upstairs was crying again while I tried to think up a fairy tale for Larry DeSantis, who bowled lane three every Monday/Wednesday/Friday, and who was beginning to feel disrespected because for three days I'd come up empty. The crying wouldn't stop for hours and was making me crazy. I screamed back. I got off the Barca recliner that I'd burst a heart-vessel haggling for at the Army-Navy, took a hammer from my toolbox, and hurled it again and again at the ceiling until my floor was covered in paint chips. Nothing stopped the baby's wailing. Nothing. I sat down again and bit my thumbnail until the skin ripped and blood formed at the cuticle. More screaming from upstairs. Finally I licked my thumb and went up there to tell the baby's parents to shut the baby the hell up. It was enough already.

A note written in green crayon was stuck to their door with packing tape.

Dear Gunnipuddy,
Take care of Tyren. We left the door open. He likes applesauce.

The note was signed *M. and C.*, initials for names that I'd forgotten seconds after hearing them the day I moved in three years ago.

I stepped into M. and C.'s apartment. No furniture, no rugs, no pictures on the walls—in this way, it looked a lot like my apartment. A baby was in the middle of the den, in a little plaid seat, bouncing up and down. When it saw me, it stopped crying. I wandered around the apartment. No toothbrushes or combs in the bathroom, no clothes in the closet. No bed in the bedroom. In the refrigerator there was applesauce behind the ketchup. I went back into the den and picked up the seat with the baby inside and carried it downstairs with the applesauce (and the ketchup) into my apartment. I put down the seat with the baby and watched for a while. I watched the baby watching me as if I knew things.

I didn't.

Here's what I learned, though: You put some applesauce on a spoon, push it into a baby's mouth, baby's going to eat. I fed it and fed it, and when it seemed full, turning its head away from the spoon, I said to Mr. Barotta's ashes, "I'll be home around ten."

"You are *not* leaving me alone with that thing," the ashes said.

But I had no choice. I had to leave for work, and so I poured the applesauce into a bowl, put it on the floor next to the baby, and left for the Breakneck Beach Bowling Centre, where I mop the bathrooms and unclog balls when they get stuck behind the pins. I've heard that working in a bowling alley is the best job for a poet, because it's mindless and doesn't sap your energy. Maybe so, but I'm no poet. This is my actual job.

Mr. Barotta had been my ninth grade music teacher. He'd had no family, and although his will had specified cremation, he hadn't taken the instructions any further. When he'd been my teacher, I hadn't liked the man. Not one bit. He'd cursed a lot and smelled like burnt coffee, and he'd seemed very, very old with those gray bushy eyebrows and creased eyes, and he'd flirt with the fourteen-year-old girls and berate us constantly about our lousy intonation, and when we played, he'd slash his baton through the air as if defending himself from an onslaught of invisible birds.

I do credit him for teaching me basic musical concepts. That, he did. "A whole note is four fucking beats. A half note is two fucking beats." Or he'd say, "When you see a fermata, look at Barotta." Then he'd grin as if all of his years spent on this planet had made him wise and cunning.

His funeral had been held next to where I did laundry anyway, and it was between the casket and the row of empty bridge chairs that the funeral director overheard me telling one of his clerical staff that Mr. Barotta had been my teacher. Suddenly, he—the funeral director—was all smiles, offering me spring water with lemon. So because I had history with the deceased—besides playing second-chair clarinet, I'd been on the Carwash Committee—and since otherwise his remains would be buried behind the crematorium next to people nobody cared for, I said okay, I'll take the stupid ashes, though I wasn't going to be suckered into paying for an urn. Mr. Barotta wasn't a man to keep in an urn anyway. He had driven a '78 Duster, and even our band uniform was nothing but blue jeans and a used white t-shirt with a logo drawn by some student from years past who'd won the School Spirit contest.

"But in a beautiful urn," the funeral director said, "the dead feel respected."

"I'll be back in an hour," I said. I went next door to get my clothes from the dryer, drove home, and dug around in the drawer of my night table for the Reel Catch fishing-tackle box. That box—hard plastic, sturdy, with a dependable clasp— had been given to me years before by a Reel Catch fishing-tackle representative one morning when my dad and I were out on the fishing pier. Long ago, I'd used up all the Reel Catch tackle. None of it ever caught one damn fish. So then I'd used it to store condoms, bought when I was young and optimistic, but I never caught any women, either. The box was cursed, I'd like to think, but more likely it was me—I wasn't any good at landing things. I took out the condoms, which had expired anyway, returned to the funeral home carrying the Reel Catch box, and in went the ashes, and there you have it.

You can't just put somebody's ashes back in your night table, so I set the Reel Catch box on a wooden dresser that had followed me from place to place and eventually to my apartment here on Talmadge Road, next to the prosthetic supply shop. I kept the dresser in the den, covering a fist-sized hole in the drywall left by an old tenant.

The next morning, I awoke to Mr. Barotta's ashes yelling at me from the other room: "Tremolo! Largo! Andante! Pianissimo!" I went into the den and looked at the Reel Catch box. The remains of my music teacher said, "What the hell are *you* doing here?"

Mr. Barotta's ashes began giving me advice. Often, his advice wasn't any good and bordered on the criminal. Usually, I ignored him. But yesterday, I'd been fed up already—what with the writer's block and the baby's screaming—and so when Mr. Barotta's ashes told me for the millionth time that I was sure to die shivering and alone, I sprang up from my kitchen chair so fast it fell over backwards, landing with a *thuck* on the linoleum, and stomped over to the dresser.

"I'll scatter you over the beach," I said to the ashes. "I swear, if that's the only peaceful—"

"Comrade," the ashes had said, "how about I scatter *you* over the beach?"

As soon as I stepped inside the Bowling Centre, I heard Larry DeSantis calling my name. I was at his lane and full of apologies before he said a word.

"I'm having a killer time working with the handlebar moustache," I said.

"But it's got to have that," Larry said, and subjected me to his secret handshake that I hadn't begun to decode, leaving my wrist sore, a layer of his sweat on my palm. "The moustache is my trademark."

Larry is a bread deliveryman done working for the day by ten a.m., and probably had been here since we opened. Leagues hadn't started yet, so there was just Larry and the other regulars, guys with their own shoes and balls named after girls they met once on a bus or in Radio Shack. We stick the regulars in the same lanes every day so that they feel part of something bigger than themselves.

"I need another day," I told Larry.

"Why, Gunnipuddy? Why is mine taking so long?"

Something I'd have liked to know. I was either on the verge of something or the verge of nothing. It felt the same. "Tomorrow, okay?"

"What've you got so far?" he asked.

I didn't want to say I'd come up empty. So I said, "Once there lived a man who delivered bread each morning to the King and Queen, and who had the world's strongest moustache."

"And?"

"And the moustache attracted the land's most beautiful women, who all wanted his hand in marriage."

"And?"

"And so the deliveryman decided to hold a contest, and agreed to marry the winner."

"No. The deliveryman makes love to many of the women before agreeing to settle down with any one of them."

This is what happens when I improvise. "I'll keep working on it," I tell him.

I wouldn't consider myself a bowler. In the three years I've worked at the Bowling Centre, I've rolled just a handful of games and never broken a hundred. The little holes in the ball make my knuckles sore. The shoes kill my feet. Still, I can see the appeal. You get your own lane where the light isn't too bright and the air temperature's steady. The Bowling Centre isn't too loud, either, not like you'd expect, because we've got carpets on the floor and on the end walls; and anyway, that smacking sound of ball hitting pins, it's a good clean sound. It means that somebody's getting points. For the regulars like Larry, we're like their local tavern, where the faces are the same every day. And it's exercise, too, if you aren't too tight with your definitions. Exercise, plus we're on tap.

I suppose you could say that bowling's a game with clear rules and a clear goal, too, which are things that you don't find too often in life. But I don't think that's it, not really, not the root of the matter. Here's the real thing about bowling: You knock the pins down, a machine sets them up again. Knock them down, up they go. The pins you miss, the machine knocks them down for you, then sets everything right. No matter what you do, whether you throw a strike or a gutter-ball, once per frame all the pins go down, then they all come back up. You might score higher or lower on a particular day, but you never fail. You can't fail at bowling.

When I got home shortly before midnight, a gray rabbit was sitting on the lawn near my front door. Its eyes reflected red light from the prosthetic supply shop's neon sign (Arms!). Even when I came close, the rabbit just sat there. Its fur was matted and missing in patches. It looked as if it'd lost a fight with one of the raccoons that live in the dumpsters. The rabbit was blocking my way, so I nudged it aside with my shoe and opened the door. But it followed me right into the apartment.

"What?" I said to the rabbit, and closed the door, trapping us all inside. I noticed how rank the apartment smelled. I looked at the baby. Tyren seemed okay, except for the applesauce on his face.

"What?" I said again.

"You irresponsible schmuck," the rabbit said.

"Seconded," Mr. Barotta's ashes said.

I knelt down next to the baby. It made some baby noises. It didn't seem too unhappy.

"I'm here, aren't I?" I said in my defense. "I went away to work but then I came home again. That's better than M. and C. could do."

"It was wailing all night," said the rabbit. "I could hear it all the way down the block."

"Way to go, Gunnipuddy," the ashes said.

I was tired from work, and frustrated because without the fairy tales I was only a utility man. My head throbbed. I went into the kitchen and swallowed three ibuprofens, then returned to the den with a roll of paper towels. "Newsflash," I announced, "I don't know how to take care of kids."

"Master of the obvious," the rabbit said. "You've got to feed it. You've got to buy diapers and change them often. A baby takes constant attention. You can't just leave food out like it's a dog."

"Gunnipuddy thinks he's got a dog," Mr. Barotta's ashes sing-songed. "A little puppy. That what you think you have?"

"A poodle," the rabbit said. "A cuddly little poodle. Gunnipuddy thinks he's got himself a poodle."

The rabbit's voice was tinny and abrasive, and although I'd gotten used to the ashes by now, the ranting still reminded me of his former self hollering at the woodwinds for playing everything staccato. Anyway, the rabbit was doing a little circular hop, and the ashes were chanting raucously along with the rabbit, "A puppy, a puppy, a—"

"Shut up, you stupid rabbit," I said. "Shut up, you stupid ashes." With a square of paper towel, I wiped the baby's face. It pulled back and started shrieking just like I'd always heard it doing upstairs. From inches away, the noise pierced straight into my skull. "Are you both going to sit around and make fun," I said, "or are you going to help? Shit, Mr. Barotta, you could be in the ground right now, staring at bugs all day." This appeared to sober him up. "Now, you two watch this baby while I get some diapers from the Wawa."

I took a fourth ibuprofen and went to the Wawa even though it was five blocks farther than the 7-Eleven, because the woman who works the register could stop the earth from spinning. If I were to make up a fairy tale about myself, she'd co-star.

"Hi, Gunnipuddy," she said when I walked in.

I waved, but nothing was how it looked. Jillian didn't know me at all. I'd been coming in there for months when finally I said to her, My name's Gunnipuddy. Can you say my name when I walk in? And she'd said, I'll try and remember, and then we had practiced, I went out and came in again and she said it, my name. Then we repeated it twice.

But today I was a different man. I had Huggies in my arms.

"How old's your baby?" she asked, her eyes wide.

"Beats me."

"How do you mean?" she asked.

"I mean, he can't talk yet. So I don't know how old he is." I was joking with her, only there were so many parts missing, things she'd need to have known, that it was hopeless. So I just paid, not looking up again from the conveyer belt, and left with the Huggies. The good part about liking a woman like Jillian was that I knew I'd get another chance with her tomorrow or the next day. The register can't make change by itself.

That first night with Tyren I learned that you aren't born knowing how to change a diaper, or knowing how to make a baby stop its nonsense. I could see why M. and C. gave up. There went one a.m., two a.m., three a.m. When the baby finally stopped complaining and fell asleep around four, I was wide awake, feeling like I had to make use of the middle of the night. The thing about writing fairy tales, though, is that you can't force them. You can't just write words on paper and expect them to be the right words. You need to spend time listening to Aerosmith. You need to get out your clarinet and play "Stars and Stripes Forever," or watch brawny men sell juicers and knives on television, or throw a Superball so hard that it hits the floor then ceiling then floor then ceiling then floor before you catch it. But all of that shit is off-limits if it wakes the baby.

"You won't believe this," Larry DeSantis said, and grabbed my wrist, forcing me into an extra-long handshake, bending my hand into baffling positions. "I mean, there's no believing it, so don't even try. You look like hell."

I did. Fifty-six diapers had come and gone. Four extra-large jars of applesauce. A week, but it might have been a month or five years or ten minutes. I'd stopped shaving, and yesterday my boss said that I smelled like a carcass. Driving home from work, I'd fallen asleep at an intersection and woken up to a UPS man tapping on my windshield. For a week I'd been scratching my hairline until it bled, and so when I lifted my head from the steering wheel, the wheel was all crusty. When I got home, I was feeling so tired and lonely—I had never felt so alone before, even with the ashes and a rabbit and a baby under my roof—that I actually bawled, until Mr. Barotta's ashes told me to stop being such a pussy.

"I met a girl last night," Larry was saying, "the most beautiful woman I ever saw. Green eyes like celery. Skin like ivory. And her name's Agatha, same as in the fairy tale."

That fairy tale had taken a superhuman level of concentration, sitting in the Barca, getting ideas during the quiet hours of 4-6 a.m., paging through *The Complete Fairy Tales of the Brothers Grimm Volume I.* That's my book. What I mean is, except for that book, I'm not a reader. I'm more like the kids who hang outside my apartment blasting T-Jerky, and who might know every lyric by this one local thug with a hit record, but who hardly are interested in music.

When Larry was a kid, my story went, he received a terrible gash on his face trying to defend a man and wife from a knife-wielding lunatic. Ashamed when the gash left a jagged sprawling scar, as soon as Larry was able he grew a moustache that covered nearly his entire face. Still, for years he kept to himself, until one day some very tiny people took up residence inside Larry's handlebar moustache. These people had fairy dust that would make Larry irresistible to women. (This was a calculated risk as to whether Larry would get pissed off because it was the dust, and not him, exactly, that made the women crazy about him).

Anyway, the fairy dust resulted in lots of sex for Larry, and talk of his sexual prowess spread across the land. Only one woman in the kingdom, however, managed to capture Larry's heart. Agatha. She urged him to shave off his moustache, because her own father and mother had been killed by a moustache-wearing lunatic. When Larry refused, Agatha put a sleep-inducing potion in his wine, and while he slept, she sheared off his moustache. When Larry awoke, he touched his lip and became mortified, knowing that his moustache housed the fairies whose dust gave him his sexual powers. He ran to the mirror and, seeing his reflection, gasped. What Larry hadn't known, because he'd worn a moustache for so long, was that the scar on his lip had come together over the years to spell the name of his true love: *Agatha.* Moreover, Larry realized, it had been Agatha's own parents who he had tried to defend all those years earlier.

The trick had been asking myself why somebody would grow a moustache like Larry's. Once I came up with the scar, things started flowing. Normally, I would have worked out what happened to the little people who lived in Larry's moustache. They had to go someplace, didn't they? And why did they have fairy dust to begin with? Ordinarily I was more careful with the loose ends. But I'd had a rough week, and something had to give.

In the end, there was true love and lots of sweaty sex. And a 300 game for Larry. They all want 300 games in their fairy tales.

"And you're saying your fairy tale came true?"

"That's what I'm saying," Larry said, and went to the bar (also the shoe-rental counter) to buy me a beer.

I'd made up a dozen or so fairy tales about customers at the Bowling Centre, but none of them had ever come true before. That was never the point, if there was a point other than doing something I had a knack for.

"You're a fortune teller, Gunnipuddy!" said Russell, a bouncer at Bazookas nightclub.

It did look that way. "Maybe," I said, and then Larry returned with my beer, handed it to me, held his right hand over the air blower, picked up his bowling ball, and rolled his ninth, tenth, and eleventh strikes. All the regulars had gathered and were shouting encouragement. Larry cradled the ball—*Angelica*—in his arms and stroked it. (With a black marker he'd crossed out some letters and added others so that now the ball sort of said *Agatha*.) You could tell he felt very tender toward that ball. He kissed it gently, then sent it down the lane so that it curved dead into the pocket. It'd be a better story, maybe, to say that while nine pins went down, the tenth pin hovered there for a moment, spinning, still standing, before finally losing to gravity. But that's not what happened. When Larry's ball hit the pocket, the ten pins exploded—that's what we call it—and dropped. The pins never had a chance.

Larry began to hyperventilate, and the guys had to ease

him onto the cool floor, where he sat with his arms around his knees, tears streaming down his face. They huddled around him and punched him on the shoulder, and said that no bowler had ever been so deserving. I sat on a bench and sipped from my beer. I wanted to be excited for Larry, except, I realized, I didn't know this man at all. Did he speak other languages? As a kid, had he been bullied? Two years I'd worked here, and yet I knew only three things about each of the regulars: name, occupation, and high score.

Obviously, others were quick to become the leading male of my fairy tales. At first it made me anxious, taking numbers and figuring out priorities.

"Ben is short and sloppy, and he drinks all day," I said to the circle of men around me. Ben, a hospital orderly, bowled lane one. "Where do I go with that?"

"Maybe he meets a barmaid?" Larry said. He'd taken some of the guys out for steaks and had returned with a splotch of sauce on his shirt.

"Maybe I meet a woman who drives a beer truck?" Ben said.

"Maybe you meet a woman at A.A.," I said. The words sounded wrong, but I pressed on. "You meet at A.A., and she owns a McDonald's franchise, and you go into business together." I jotted this down on the back of a score sheet so that I'd remember it later.

"We meet at A.A.?" He pursed his lips.

Larry asked Ben, "Do you see yourself giving up the liquor?"

"Don't ask me, ask Gunnipuddy. He's the storyteller."

Maybe I was, but I wasn't going to lie. "No. Ben's right. She drives a beer truck. Her route takes her past an old witch's hovel, where…" I looked around at the pairs of eyes straining wide at me. "I'll work on it when I get home tonight."

"What about me?" said Frank, a wedding DJ. "Am I going to end up with a hot bridesmaid or something?"

"No, me," said Russell, the bouncer.

"Russell, Russell." I chewed on the little half-pencil. "I always see you riding that stupid bicycle." I had never asked, but it had to be a DUI. "So let's think about what type of woman—"

"Money, Gunnipuddy. I need money."

My version of *The Complete Fairy Tales of the Brothers Grimm Volume I* ("The Frog King" through "The Devil's Sooty Brother") comes apart in your hands. The binding isn't any good. I stole the book from my school's library because there was talk of banning it. I didn't think that people banned books anymore, but I was wrong. Anyway, I saved them the hassle. After I stole it, for years I kept it under my mattress like a baseball glove, as if I had other kids on my team depending on me.

When I told the rabbit and Mr. Barotta's ashes that my fairy tales had been coming true, first Larry's and then Ben's and now Russell's, the rabbit said, "You're home late again."

"Idiot," Mr. Barotta's ashes added.

"The guys took me out drinking. I couldn't say no." It was true. Everyone at the bowling alley looked at me differently now that I had great powers. I'd stopped cleaning the bathrooms, but nobody said anything. Clogged toilets, nothing. Musty urinals, nothing. I just sat on a bench at the end of the alley, lane twenty-four, and guys brought me beer from the tap and Pop Tarts from the vending machines. I got the idea they loved me and feared me.

"Yesterday, Russell won five grand playing Lotto," I said, and flopped backwards onto the Barca. "It would've been an insult not to let him get me drunk."

The baby was sucking on a binky I'd bought at the Wawa.

"All I'm saying is," said the rabbit, "you've got a baby now, and you can't be—"

"Are you my wife? Is that it?" The last thing I wanted was a lecture. I wanted to be drunk and ride the high of telling fortunes or creating fortunes or whatever it was that I seemed able to do. But forces had converged against me—not only Tyren, but also the rabbit, which was supposedly watching Tyren while I was away. Yet its own pellets were everywhere, its fur was everywhere, and a place on its back that used to have fur had become infected or something and was red and dotted with pus. I shook my head in disgust. "I've got to get to work."

"It's three a.m. and you just came from work," the rabbit said. "You don't have to go back there."

"No, I mean, I've got to write more fairy tales." I went into my bedroom with my book so that I could get some work done for the guys at the alley where, unlike here, I was appreciated.

In the morning, things were more civil. I sat on the floor with Tyren in a square of sunlight and fed him sweet potatoes and apples. Despite what M. and C. had written on their note, I found that Tyren wasn't a fussy eater. You could mix leftovers from all sorts of jars—peas, pears, pumpkin, creamed chicken—and he'd slurp it up. Also, if you put him on his stomach, he'd roll over onto his back. A good trick. And he'd laugh whenever you hung tube socks over your ears and said *blagablagablagablaga*.

"You must be a hero at the alley," the rabbit said, watching me and the baby from across the room.

"Work's been satisfying." I tried to stand on my head, because Tyren liked seeing me upside-down, but the hard floor irritated my sore scalp.

"You're a man of special powers, Gunnipuddy."

I didn't want to admit what I was about to admit, so I reached for a bottle of baby food and pretended that I couldn't unscrew the cap.

"Need help with that, Hercules?" asked Mr. Barotta's ashes.

I twisted open the bottle.

"I don't think it's me," I said to the rabbit and to Mr. Barotta's ashes. "None of my fairy tales ever came true before. I think this baby is special." We all looked at Tyren, who was looking at me, but only because I was holding the food. "Yeah, I'm pretty sure it's a godlike baby. I think it might be God. Or something just as important. So don't kill it accidentally while I'm at work."

The baby piped up: "No, I'm not very important. If you don't consider the fate of the world very important."

"Oh, shit," the ashes said.

"Baby's first words," said the rabbit.

I put down the bottle I'd just opened and watched Tyren, waiting for some elaboration. Outside, the sun was barely up, yet the kids were already blasting T-Jerky.

"I'll fill you in," Tyren said, "while you change my diaper."

I grabbed him under my arm and carried him like a football into my bedroom where I kept the Huggies. Now that he could speak, I felt that I had better do a thorough job cleaning him, applying the cream, making sure that the tape didn't pinch.

Anyway, Tyren had completely exaggerated. It wasn't anything like the fate of the world. It was just a dumb car accident that I could prevent, a fender-bender at an intersection across the street from the Wawa. The drivers were of religions and ethnicities that had spent several thousand years hating each other, so maybe you could argue that if the accident had occurred, it would have worsened the tension between two communities, and that maybe this accident would have been the straw that broke, etc., and that battles would be waged, wars fought; that this particular accident, as non-political and, well, accidental, as it might be, occurred for reasons far more cosmic than I could understand, the one accident that had to be prevented at any cost. Or maybe the incident was more symbolic, like if these two people's crisis could be averted, then blah blah. Or maybe Tyren was way off base, being a baby.

He told me the how's and where's and when's of the accident, which pissed me off because the *when* was only thirty minutes from *then*. I put Tyren in the crib I'd bought him at Baby Depot, ran outside to my car, and sped to the Wawa to ask Jillian to a movie.

Not the best timing, maybe, with the clock ticking and all, but something about the urgency I was feeling gave me a surge of adrenaline. Do it now, I said to myself. Right now.

Twenty-eight minutes later, I didn't care whether I fumbled the fate of the world or not, because Jillian had said no, fucking no, she preferred not to meet me at the Regal Cinema for a movie. So fuck the world, I was thinking.

And yet I was thinking this from a position standing outside the Wawa, eight-thirty on a Friday morning, right where Tyren had told me to be, and overhead the traffic light suddenly started blinking yellow on all four sides, and there came the '86 Ford Taurus and the '88 Honda Civic, just as Tyren had said, and since I was the only one there who knew what was going to happen, I went into the middle of the street and stood with my hand outstretched like a traffic cop's in front of the Honda, which I assumed had better brakes than the Taurus. The car screeched to a stop. The driver growled something and gave me the finger.

I went around to the driver's window, and he rolled it down. He had an immense gray beard and round green eyes, and I thought how easy it would be to write a fairy tale about him.

"I'm taking a survey," I said. "Do you drink Coke—"

At that moment, the Ford Taurus puttered through the intersection and was gone, my mission accomplished.

"Or is Pepsi more your thing?"

The man gritted his teeth and roared the engine, sending the car forward—over my feet, crushing bones—and into the intersection. Long after the car was out of sight, I kept howling.

When I refused to stay overnight at Saint Memorial's on account of the baby, the surgeon said that I was being-a-difficult-patient, that I must reconsider. Then he left my room and returned with a form stating that I was being noncompliant with my physician's orders, that I released him and the institution from any liability. He sent me home with prescription painkillers, a pamphlet (*Caring for Your Wound*), and a walker. I didn't get home until ten p.m. When I told everybody about what'd happened, the rabbit said, "Then it's time to leave."

"But I just came home," I said.

"Me. I'm leaving. So open the door."

"Why're you leaving?"

"I'm all done here. My job was to make sure you bought Huggies and took care of the baby."

"I still don't know how to take care of a baby."

"I know. But you're learning, which means that my job's done."

"You have only one job?" I wasn't being very considerate of that rabbit—I could tell he needed the outdoors, some grass, dumpsters to rummage through. Yet it felt wrong for him to abandon not only the baby, but an invalid still numb from foot surgery and high on painkillers. "Why can't you have more than one job?"

"Why? Because I'm a fucking rabbit. And about that girl," the rabbit said. "It's just a rejection. No biggie. Ask her out again."

"You think?" Jillian had heard me cursing in the intersection and, seeing my smashed feet, called for an ambulance. Maybe it was the beginning of something.

"Sure. Isn't that right, Mr. Barotta's Ashes?"

"In two-four time," the ashes said, "the quarter note gets one goddamned beat. In six-eight time, the eighth note gets one goddamned beat."

"Just don't stalk her or anything," the rabbit said. "Don't get creepy on her. And remember that the kid always comes first. Now let me out. I want out."

After the rabbit left, I picked up Tyren and put him on my lap in the recliner, but he was being all wiggly, so I put him on the floor where there were some old milk cartons I'd saved for him. My feet killed, but I wasn't supposed to take more pills for another four hours. In my head, I starting writing a fairy tale about Bridget, who rents the bowling shoes, about how she found a rich architect to run off with. But it didn't feel right. The words in my head felt as if they'd been written by someone who didn't know a damn thing.

"This won't come true, will it?" I asked Tyren.

He looked up. "No."

"Why not?" I pictured the clogged toilets I'd been ignoring for over a week. And how even though I never promised anyone anything, there'd be hell to pay at the Bowling Centre if I were just a utility man again.

"You're a loser, Gunnipuddy, and yet you took care of me without hesitation. That was some good work, so I made you a hotshot for a while."

"Aha!" yelled Mr. Barotta's ashes from across the room. "I *knew* Gunnipuddy had no talent of his own!"

Tyren ignored the ashes. "You took in a baby even though you're a totally unfit father. You're a good man, Gunnipuddy."

And those were the last words the baby ever said until he was eighteen months old. Turns out, except for when he was God, Tyren was a late talker.

Not long ago, I took Tyren to a little park. Afterward, I was pushing the stroller up the hill back toward the apartment when the owner of the prosthetic supply shop saw how badly I still hobbled and waved me in. He was a thin old man, all teeth and joints, and he'd always seemed harmless. But I'd never even said two words to him.

"Name's Fink," he said, once I was inside his shop. Along the walls were various wheelchairs and crutches and walkers, and on shelves were hand- and arm- and foot- and leg-looking devices, though none of them looked very much like hands, arms, etc.—just enough to suggest what they were meant to represent. On a shelf running along the window was information on various products—colorful pamphlets, or what my dad would have called, *literature*.

"Gunnipuddy," I said.

"Apartment next door?"

"That's right."

He knelt down. "Who's the little one?"

I told him, and we both looked in the stroller at Tyren, who was sleeping, silent, giving the wrong impression of himself.

"Mister Gunnipuddy, you just sit right here and take the weight off those feet. You make yourself comfortable. What size shoe do you wear?"

I told him, and he went into the back room and then reappeared carrying two cardboard boxes. Inside each box was a soft foot-sole-looking contraption that fits into your shoes if you've got fucked-up feet. I'm making it sound simpler than it is—he rattled off some words, *plastoform* and *purolon-urethane* and other things I've forgotten—but that's the gist. The point is, those contraptions that he put into my lap so that I could feel them, they were soft. Not squishy, though. Supportive.

Fink took them from my lap and kneaded one into each shoe. I put on my shoes again, stood, and, using the stroller for support, took a few steps.

"Well?" Fink said. "Better?"

"I'm walking on cotton," I told him. Not true, but each step wasn't excruciating, either.

"My diabetics swear by them." He nodded sagely and put me on a payment plan. Still leaning on the baby's stroller, but feeling less pain than I had in months, I headed toward the door. When I'd gotten to the doorway, Fink called out, "Behaves himself, doesn't he?"

Tyren had been asleep the whole time.

"He's curious," I said. "Always into stuff." I smiled then, because just that morning I'd been making grilled-cheese sandwiches when Tyren got his hands on the Reel Catch box and opened the clasp. The ashes spilled right out onto the rug. I got mad for a moment, cursing like Mr. Barotta would have, while Tyren stared up at me with big eyes and new teeth. I vacuumed the mess and made a mental note to empty the vacuum bag in a nice place, like in the grade-school playground, or maybe on the beach the way I'd sometimes threatened. I rinsed off the Reel Catch box and put it back inside my night table, deciding right then that next time I went to the Wawa, I'd buy a pack of condoms to keep in the box. The way I saw it, it was time to find a girl—Jillian, maybe, or somebody else—and prevent starting a family together.

"I'll bet he's a bright little boy," Fink the shop-owner said, and came over for another look. "Is he a bright boy?"

I'm happy to report: this baby's average.

ONE LAST GOOD TIME

Caught in the ragged rocks of the Breakneck Beach seawall was a dead man whose name had been Vinnie Tucci, whose occupation had been driving a school bus, whose hobbies had included fishing (mackerel in spring, blues in summer, bass till Halloween) and college football (preseason through glorious New Year's Day), and whose wife Carla had spent the night seated at the kitchen table of their split-level, mug of coffee cooling in her hands, holding out hope that Vinnie hadn't done anything stupider than he'd already done, but was instead fucking her sister Amanda's lights out at a motel in Asbury or Bradley Beach or Sea Girt and would turn up later, rumpled and reeking of woman. Yesterday, Vinnie had kept the number 2 bus that was filled with second through fourth graders, kept it so long that newscasters were calling it a *hijacking* and a *kidnapping*. And while it was disappointing that Vinnie apparently had chosen to spend these last hours of freedom apart from his own wife, Carla also knew from the police outside that the moment his car pulled up to the curb he'd be yanked into custody for a long, long time. So if Vinnie was showing Amanda one last good time in a thirty-a-night motel before coming home and facing the music, then Carla would forgive this last sin.

Carla hadn't seen Vinnie since before he'd left for his route yesterday morning, when he'd eaten four eggs that she'd served runny because he liked them hard, without toast because it'd gotten moldy, since he'd slurped down Wawa brand orange juice from its carton, grimacing from the pulp, then belching like a frog. He glanced at the wristwatch she'd bought him back when she bought him presents for no reason but love.

Last thing he said to Carla: "Hell, I'm late."

Last thing she said to him: who could remember?—though it hadn't been about her sister Amanda, despite every morning beginning with that thought. Every day, the force of it—the affair—hit Carla afresh, hard, like morning sickness, not only in her gut but in her chest, her joints, her throat. Everywhere. During the day she would imagine their house the scene of fierce drama: demands and ultimatums, swearing, dish-smashing, photograph-tearing. So far, however, all she had done was to buy his juice with pulp. Undercook his eggs.

Now it was 2:30 a.m., twenty hours after Vinnie had left for work, and although Carla didn't know it yet, the seawall had him. The seawall: twelve feet high and nearly as wide, layers of jagged granite held in place by gravity and cement, designed decades earlier by the Army Corps of Engineers to protect the homes of those wealthy enough to influence state politics. The wall, however, was no match for the storm surges that once or twice a decade would leave homes waist-deep in seawater. Over time the wealthy moved to towns with wider beaches, and people like Vinnie Tucci's father moved to Breakneck Beach because property uninsurable against flooding came cheap. Here Vinnie had lived all his twenty-nine years.

He was dead, now—bashed head, then unconsciousness, then lungs full of seawater—and the force of last night's moon tide had stuffed him tightly into the wall. At high tide, 9:34 p.m., the waves were crashing against the wall and spraying cars driving along Ocean Avenue. No way was Vinnie going to get dislodged. He was there when the rats became curious, was there when a flashlight shined on his salty face at 4:18 a.m., scattering the rats, when Tark Healey, the cop holding the flashlight, dropped the flashlight, staggered back a step, and said, "Jesus Aitch."

You marry one sister, then begin to love the other. There's your problem. A dozen years ago, you flunked out of high school, worked for a moving company until your knuckles became gnarled and swollen, then began driving the elementary school bus, your old bus, the number 2. Same oversized steering wheel, same smell of vinyl. Pay: three-fifty a week. Easy work, home by five. When you were young, the bus driver would creep the front tires over a speed bump, then accelerate quickly so the rear would bounce into the air, giving the kids a thrill. Now, this is something you do.

You knew Carla Van Sickle since the fourth grade, when she was all elbows and knees. Fast-forward fifteen years, and it's you behind the wheel, she in the school cafeteria slinging hamburgers and chicken patties. After you drop the kids off and before she goes inside to face a hundred pounds of meat, you light up cigarettes out by the basketball court. Carla isn't skinny anymore. She has become curvy. Her breasts are the sort that draw glances, and she has taken to wearing v-neck collars that are simultaneously proper and suggestive. Her eyes are big and blue, her voice lush, her laugh unrestrained. Standing with her outside the school feels as if you're cutting class together.

When you're with Carla—smoking cigarettes by the basketball hoop, or messing around in your apartment over the laundromat—her sister Amanda is fourteen. She isn't even on your radar screen.

In five years, though, after you've married Carla and saved

money and purchased a small house, after Carla tells you the reason she's been awful lately is because you've knocked her up, then Amanda Van Sickle is nineteen and you're cooked. While your wife is fat and moody, Amanda is lithe and living in your house temporarily because one lease has ended and she has yet to sign another. And though this little house and this pregnant wife are just the dream you've dreamt, now that the dream is real—mortgage payments that won't ever end, Carla's mood swings, her *hemorrhoids*, for Christ sakes—your life becomes dominated by two thoughts: You must make love to Amanda. And Carla must not find out.

And make no mistake, Amanda *is* interested.

Very attractive, she said, referring to you. Then she nodded and said *very* again.

The situation: Amanda in your home, after work. The three of you at the kitchen table eating supper, drinking beer. A peaceful evening. You complaining about your crow's feet, which had been bothering you lately whenever you looked in the mirror. "Look at me," you said. "I'm an old man!"

"Well, *I* think lines around the eyes are attractive on a man," your wife Carla said. "Shows he's been smiling." Then to Amanda she said, "Aren't those lines attractive?"

And Amanda said—

She said *that*, then nodded, then said it again. And once she did, it was all over but the when and the how. Now, months later, your wife is large and growing. You've heard that some men go wild with horniness over their pregnant wives. These men don't have Amanda Van Sickle living in their homes. Amanda, with long legs and hair down to her ass. Whose full lips you need to suck, whose sly gaze makes your neck go goose-pimpled, whose voice purrs—you swear—like an engine.

The when: New Year's Day. Carla was visiting her mother,

who'd busted her hip and was lying alone at the nursing home. Carla didn't even like her mother. Called her a superstitious old bird. But you shouldn't have to be alone on New Year's Day, Carla said. "Not unless you're watching ten hours of football," she added, and left. Which explains the how: you, alone with Amanda, a little hung over from two bottles of sparkling wine that you and Amanda had split while Carla drank non-alcoholic cider. Amanda in pink sweatpants and a plain white T-shirt and no bra in sight.

Miami and Nebraska were into the second quarter of the Orange Bowl. A small television squawked in the kitchen. In the den, you and Amanda were on the sofa talking resolutions, her feet on your lap.

"Don't you think that *happiness* is maybe too broad?" you asked.

She scooted closer, the backs of her thighs now on your lap, the bulk of her against your hip. "But that's what I want," she said. "It's what I resolve to get."

"And how do you intend on doing that?" you asked, raising your eyebrows, daring her.

Her gaze locked on yours. "Do you really want to know?"

You said that you did.

"You'd better be sure, buster," she said. The television went to commercial. Something about a carpet sale. One day only, better act fast. Amanda took your hand and guided it under her T-shirt.

Question: How could Vinnie tell Amanda that he loved her, loved her hard, loved her to the point that he was willing to give up everything—his wife, his son or daughter—*Amanda's* niece or nephew—how could he say he was going to give up all this, the family, the house, even the town that meant everything to him, and not remember that it was her goddamn birthday?

Answer: he wasn't going to give up anything. It was a

sign, or like Amanda's mother would say, a *portent*. Amanda and Carla had lived with all of their mother's portents—houseplants dying even when you watered them, candles winking out for no reason, squirrels raiding the bird feeder. And while Amanda didn't necessarily believe that a squirrel eating out of your feeder foretold trouble, even she could see that a man willing to enter your body but not willing to commit your birthday to his memory made for one bad portent.

And Vinnie was leaving clues, or portents, or whatever, as large as billboards. Like the Trojans Amanda found in his glove box, the stupid idiot, as if Carla never went in there for mints. And because of Vinnie's clues, or maybe in spite of them, Carla knew what went on between Vinnie and Amanda. This was terrible, Carla knowing, terrible that Amanda *knew* that Carla knew, and terrible that despite all this knowing going on, the three of them still lived under one roof, acting as if nobody knew anything. The air got thick enough to choke on. Yet Vinnie didn't even notice. He thought he was still getting away with something.

Like yesterday afternoon, in the lull before Vinnie's route, when he had shown up at the motel with flowers. Amanda had laid them on the night table, and she and Vinnie had made love to the fragrance of lilies and hyacinths. Afterwards, outside in the parking lot of the Cheshire Motel, Vinnie had taken the bouquet from Amanda and headed toward the dumpster.

"Hey, wait a minute," she said, following him. "What the hell are you doing?"

"The flowers are for here," he said. "You can't be bringing them home."

"They don't have to be from *you*, you know."

"Nah," he said. "Too risky."

"It wouldn't be the first time a man has given me flowers on my birthday," she said, though this wasn't true.

He turned to face her, his eyes bright. He grinned. "Well, shit, Amanda. Happy birthday."

Bottom line: if your lover forgot your birthday, if you found yourself accepting flowers from a man and having to throw them into the dumpster an hour later, then your lover didn't give a damn about you. Despite Vinnie's words (there had been a *lot* of words, though not as many lately) there was no future with Vinnie. No, Amanda had messed up worse than she'd even imagined, and she came to see that if there was a relationship she could save, it was not with Vinnie, but with her sister.

Vinnie stood there, believing that because of his toothy grin, all was forgiven and forgotten, that in a day or two he and Amanda would be back at this same motel, or another one like it. He thought he had everything under control. "But you still can't keep the flowers, baby," he said, and batted her on the ass with the bouquet, hard enough to sting.

"Hey!" She grabbed the flowers from Vinnie. "Hey, you asshole..." She started smacking him with them—on the arms, the back. Vinnie held out his arms to stop the blows. He was laughing. She felt tears of shame coming to her eyes, but he thought they were playing. The more he laughed, the harder she hit him with the flowers. She tried to hurt him, but he kept blocking her swipes. He kept laughing. So she stopped hitting him. Her breath labored and face hot, she walked to the dumpster and threw in the bouquet.

She turned to face Vinnie. "I'm coming clean with Carla."

Vinnie shook his head. "You know you aren't going to do that."

"She already knows," she said, "but I'm coming clean anyway."

"We've been through all this. And what's best for us—"

"Shut up, Vinnie. Listen to me: I'm going to tell her. Count on it."

They stood in the motel's parking lot, the March wind whipping an American flag like in old war movies on TV. She meant it, coming clean, and she could see that Vinnie knew she meant it, because his face went pale, and he wouldn't look at her, and even when he started talking, he had nothing to say.

At 2:50 a.m., Carla watched her sister's car pull into the driveway. The police across the street turned on their flashing lights, silently, the silent part pointless because the neighbors were awake and peering out their windows at the patrol cars and the TV news vans parked in a line, everybody trained in the business of waiting.

Now the vans began belching out men with video cameras. One of the cops crunched across the cold grass, took Amanda by the elbow, and led her to his cruiser. The police had been hoping for Vinnie, didn't expect Amanda to know anything—why would they suspect she'd been fucking Vinnie for months?—but she was a body in motion at an hour when people were supposed to be in bed. Inside the house, Carla sat at the table in her brown robe. She lit a cigarette, the fifth one today, the fifth one since last summer, because good mothers gave up smoking. When Carla's cigarette was half gone, Amanda got out of the police cruiser and came to the front door, unlocked it, slipped inside.

Amanda entered the dimly lit hallway crying, pathetic, because in no way should she be as worried as Carla, who wasn't crying. Amanda didn't seem surprised to see her sister awake in the kitchen. "Nobody's heard anything?" she asked—her way, perhaps, of letting Carla know she hadn't slept with Vinnie tonight after all.

"Where've you been?" Carla said.

Amanda looked out the window, at the police cars. Four of them. "Christ, I was out driving. For hours. I think I'm losing my mind."

"Stop it right there—don't make this about you. It isn't about you."

"No." Amanda was looking out the window. "No, I guess it isn't." Lately, her gaze avoided Carla's stomach. "So are you all right?"

"Me? I'm not the one who hijacked a bus." She took a drag from her cigarette. "I mean, who would do that? How could he not realize the consequences?"

"That's Vinnie for you." Amanda came over to the table and took a cigarette from the pack, lit it. "It's like that stupid sunburn he'd get from being out on his boat and not wearing sun block." Vinnie used to charter a motorboat, summers, for extra cash. That was before the ocean got ruined with raw sewage and red tides, before syringes and colostomy bags washed ashore and a plague of filth killed the fish and drove away the weekend fishermen.

"God, it isn't like that at all," Carla said. Then, Carla would take Vinnie into their bedroom and rub cool cream on his beet-colored shoulders, his ears, the back of his neck. "How could you think it's anything like that?"

"All I mean is that he never thinks." She was over by the window again. "He actually told me once that he was immune to sunburn."

This was what people talk about after a funeral, Carla thought. The moments that make you shake your head and say, *The man was something else.* "But he isn't immune, is he?"

Amanda sighed deeply. She mashed her cigarette in the ashtray. "The fucking idiot. I swear. . . ."

Carla watched her sister: wet-eyed, snotty, petulant as if stood up for prom. As if a bad sunburn were the worst thing in this world. All I did, Carla thought, was invite you into my house. You were between leases. I asked you in. And now all of this. She placed the coffee mug down on the tabletop. "You know what? Maybe you'd better not be calling Vinnie names, okay? Just remember whose husband he is."

"Oh?" Amanda looked straight at Carla. "Well, your husband says he loves me."

The baby kicked.

Scenario: you're cheating on your pregnant wife with her sister, and it's becoming more certain that in your not-too-distant future lies a fucking awful divorce where she keeps the baby from you. You're in Breakneck Beach, population 6,000, where everyone will know what you've done. People may not know *you*, but this thing about you they'll know, because scandal travels. You're driving from the elementary school with a busload of precious cargo. You are sleepless from worry, knowing that when you get home today everything will change, because Amanda meant what she said about telling Carla. You've gotten pretty good at reading Amanda's eyes, and yesterday at the motel those eyes had been angry and willful.

The problem with Amanda is that she wants a clear conscience, even if she—like you—doesn't deserve one. She has threatened you before, but only in the abstract. *I should tell her. I've got to tell her. I need to tell her.* Never was it, *I'm going* to. Yesterday was different. She'd meant it. Suddenly, she believes in honesty above all else. How about telling the truth back on New Year's Day? How about saying, *If we fuck, I'm going to tell my sister.* Where was the honesty then? So in the freezing parking lot of that god-awful motel, Amanda says that your only hope, if you are ever to be together, is to come clean. She's wrong. Coming clean offers no hope. You and she could never be together in Breakneck Beach. You'd have to move far away with her, and then you'd lose not only your wife and the house and your unborn child, but Amanda, too, because when you came down to it, Amanda wouldn't ever be satisfied living someplace faraway with you. She's got it too easy now, gossiping with the mothers of her high school friends while sanding and painting their fingernails, their toenails. At night, coaxing free drinks from the bartenders who are the older brothers of boys she destroyed in high school. Sleeping with other men when she cares to. You don't know this for a fact, but you have to assume. She's sexy and young and hits the local bars frequently, so what do you expect? You don't mind, much, though it's further evidence that she wouldn't ever be happy with you, *exclusively* you, starting life from scratch in some strange town.

"Look," you said to her yesterday, after your voice had come back to you in the motel parking lot, "we'll keep this a secret until the baby comes. Then we'll tell her, and plan our future together." You've said this before, and some days you mean it, and usually it stops the debate.

"She already *knows*, Vinnie," Amanda said, shaking her head at your stupidity. "I'm just coming clean."

Despite what Amanda might think, your wife *doesn't* know. She suspects. But suspecting is a world away from knowing, because when you suspect something bad, you can still hold onto the hope—however remote—that you're wrong. Carla could choose to misread the evidence, to assemble the pieces so as not to fit. This is the only gift you're able to give your wife right now, the right to keep on deceiving herself until the baby is born. And now Amanda was out to deny your wife that gift.

All last night you thought, *Here it comes.* The three of you were at home, watching a program where detectives risked their lives, and every time Amanda glanced at you, or at Carla, you gritted your teeth, bracing yourself. Astonishing, Amanda's power over you. She, too, must have felt it, because all night she kept clearing her throat, as if to speak. Once again, it was only a question of when. Of how.

You barely slept, and after this morning's route you spent hours downtown killing time because you were afraid to go home. Now, driving the afternoon route, you are exhausted.

Yesterday's conversation with Amanda replays in your mind. Right at this moment Amanda could be at home with Carla, revealing every secret she swore to uphold. You're not paying attention as you should, and when the brown dog runs into the road, it's just a blur.

You hit it squarely, not noticing it until it bounces off the front fender as if the bus were made of rubber, and now the dog is in the air, turning, and then landing in the gutter by the curb. The bus barely reacts, a slight shimmy. Not until you're thirty feet down the road does a girl happen to look out the back window.

"A dog!" she yells. "The bus hit a dog!"

Through the rearview, you see it's a big one—a retriever, or a setter. Unmoving. A woman runs toward the street. She's looking at you. No—she's looking at the rear of the bus, not at you, but you could swear she's looking into your eyes with shock and disappointment. You should stop the bus. But then you will have on your hands a busload of children weeping over a dead dog, and this woman, and then the police, who will take a report. There will be explanations to parents, to the school. Can you face this now? Today? In the few seconds of this deliberation, you are farther down the road and away from the scene. By not deciding, a decision has been made.

So this, you think, is how it begins.

You keep driving, missing one of your stops, then another. The children are running up and down the aisle, no longer crying about *the dog, the dog, the dog* but rather that they *want to go home.*

"Sit down, kids!" you yell. It is impossible to think with all of this carrying on. "Sit down!"

Most of them listen. One of the bigger students, a fourth grader with sandy hair, comes and stands next to you. "We have to go home now," he says, his voice shaky but controlled. He's on this bus every day, but you never gave him a second thought.

"I have a gun," you tell him, "and I'll use it if I have to. Now sit down."

This is highly effective. You don't have a gun, but word spreads as if you do, and momentarily all of the children are in their seats imagining what it is like to be shot. There are tears and sniffles, a few soft moans. You only wanted them to be still, however, not petrified, and so you take them to the McDonald's drive-through. "Thirty hamburgers," you say, and a staticky voice mutters a price. You take bills out of your wallet and pay for the hamburgers. You drive to the next window and receive three warm white bags.

"Here," you say to the girl seated behind you, feeling both benevolent and ridiculous. "Pass these out."

Now the bus smells of fast food, and this is soothing to you and the children.

You drive east, toward Ocean Avenue. It is still too early for a parent to become concerned and begin the inevitable chain of phone calls: parent to school, school to police. You hadn't planned any of this, but now that you've done it, kept the number 2 bus, you're glad at least to be forcing a fate having nothing to do with your wife or her sister, with secrets or broken trust. You aren't waiting anymore for your sister-in-law to tell her sister that the two of you are in love and have been to bed together more than thirty times.

This bus ride will end in arrest, or worse, and you will lose your job and your freedom and your money, your wife and Amanda both, and while each of these individual losses could tear a hole in your gut, the broad loss anesthetizes you. By keeping the number 2, you have reduced your options to the point where you feel comforted by the one thing you *can* do. You can drive the bus. You have a tank of fuel and well-fed passengers. Before you hit that dog your mind was everywhere. Not anymore. You've turned North on Ocean Avenue, have passed Rex's Italian Sausages and the place you still think of as the fishing pier even though it's been an amusement park for some years now. On your right just north of the pier starts the seawall. On your left are houses painted cheerful blues and yellows and greens, most with second-story decks, many with American flags flapping out front. The road ahead leads out of town.

If you stay on this road, the police will spot you. You imagine them shooting out your tires. Shooting you out of the driver's seat. When the road forks a few miles later, forcing you to choose either to stay on the road or exit to Sandy Hook, you exit. Sandy Hook is a peninsula jutting out from the coastline toward New York Harbor. Summers, pale New Yorkers flood to the national recreation area. But it's off-season, and the kiosk is unmanned, the parking lot empty. You drive toward the beach, where the parking lot ends. Where your ride ends.

When the bus is spotted, you'll be hunted down like a dog. No one will care that you bought hamburgers for the children. You briefly imagine that after you've paid your debt—fines? Probation? A year, two in jail?—you can move away but still see your child sometimes. Weekends, or once a month, or whatever Carla or some judge might allow. You can find a quiet town up in Maine or Vermont where the lakes are loaded with bass. But you know that won't happen.

"Kids, listen up," you say. You have everyone's attention. Even those whose heads were wobbling a moment ago have snapped awake. "Soon your mothers and fathers will come to take you home. But only if you sit in your seats and don't make a sound. Remember, I have a gun. Does everybody understand?" But who can tell? Nobody dares to move a muscle. And once the driver's door is open and you start running toward the wooden stairway that leads up and over the seawall, you don't look back.

On the beach, a wavy line of shells and seaweed and plastic bottles and jugs is being swallowed by the incoming tide. Though the sun hasn't set yet, a full moon glows red to the east. You look at your watch. By now the first calls must be coming in to school. Soon, the police will be notified, and they'll find the bus. You run south along the narrow beach, sucking cold air, the ocean on your left, the seawall on your right, the sound of sirens in the distance. (For you? Probably not yet. But maybe.) You aren't a runner, not by a long shot, and soon you're panting, your knees shaky, a wave of nausea rising. Still, you keep moving. Keep putting distance between yourself and the bus. You cover a mile, maybe more. Icy water licks your ankles. Soon there won't be any beach left. You've never felt so tired.

Back when you proposed to Carla, you actually used the word *hitched*. That was on the beach, too, not far at all from here. Low tide, warm September evening. There was the coat and tie. The down-on-one-knee. But you couldn't sustain it, the sincerity. She accepted, she cried and carried on, but even then you were disgusted that you said it like that—*hitched*—practically a smirk. Because you didn't *mean* hitched. You meant married, and you meant forever.

A few more stumbled paces as the nausea mounts. At the base of the seawall you double over and vomit on the rocks, not knowing if it's from hard running, or fear of the law, or what you've done to those children, or to Carla or Amanda. Or all of it. Despite the cold wind and surf, you're sweating, heart racing, eyes squeezed shut, hands clutching your gut. You've given up control of your body and are vomiting, and the taste of it makes you vomit some more. Behind you, close, a wave crashing. And when it hits you from behind, you lose your footing and tumble forward toward the jagged wall. You feel the smallest tap of your head against granite. A light tap, like the little rubber instrument a doctor hits your knees with. It barely even hurts, and the lights go out.

Tap, and you're dead.

Maybe Vinnie had gone a little crazy today, keeping the bus, but Amanda understood it. Understood the calming influence of an automobile even better than Vinnie did. Some, when anxious, drank liquor. Others exercised. Whenever Amanda became stressed, she got in her car and drove. Destination unimportant. She would put in a CD— lately it was a local ska band—and play it as loudly as her Mazda's speakers would allow before the bass began sizzling with distortion.

When Amanda first described her solo excursions to Vinnie, he had looked puzzled.

"But where do you go?" he asked.

"That isn't the point. You aren't going anywhere. You just…drive."

"But why?"

When she thought about it, she didn't know why. "Try it sometime," she finally said.

Amanda had been in the break room at the salon when Vinnie's face appeared on television along with the words *School Bus Hijacking*. The news coverage cut to weepy and frantic parents, to the school's thick-necked principal, then to a recap—but no bus. No children, no Vinnie. She watched a while longer, then hurried out the salon's back door. Got in her car, and drove.

She headed north on Ocean Avenue, the music blaring, unaware that she was duplicating part of Vinnie's own drive hours earlier. At the fork in the road where Vinnie had ended his drive, Amanda kept heading north, through the Highlands and Keansburg and Keyport. She drove the state roads and local streets, winding past apartments she'd never desire and houses she'd never afford, trying to give herself up fully to the music. At eleven p.m. she stopped for gasoline. At midnight, to pee. Other than that she stopped only for red lights and stop signs.

With no destination in mind, it wasn't until one a.m. that she found herself at the New York border. She considered, as Vinnie had, driving north and never returning. She could keep going: Connecticut...Maine...Quebec. But did she have the courage? In wartime, if she were a young man, would she have made the one-way drive north to begin her life again? No, she decided, and turned the car around. Headed to well-traveled territory: the ruins of Asbury Park, where everybody hoped to glimpse Bruce Springsteen and have that story to carry around; she passed Lakewood and Forked River and Egg Harbor. By now the music wasn't doing its trick anymore. She imagined Vinnie in prison. Or avoiding prison but remaining with Carla—because there would be this kid who'd maybe have Vinnie's ears, or Carla's chin, and they would see this child as a portent of better things. They would try to make a clean start because there had once been love.

Amanda turned north again and headed home—rather, to her sister's home. In a few hours the sun would be up on the morning of the third day of her twentieth year, and oh Jesus she wanted to drive anyplace but Carla's house, and yet she found herself driving there anyway.

She fumbled in her glove box for another CD. Moments later the car was full of sound. Vinnie never liked her taste in music. *You want reggae,* he once said, *I got two words for you: Bob Marley.*

"Stop it!" she said, to nobody, and stepped hard on the accelerator.

At 4:30 a.m., Tark Healey made the visit. It wasn't the first time Tark, a veteran on the force, had to deliver death. This time, however, it would be a challenge to mask the sense of righteousness in his voice. His daughter had been on the number 2.

He waved aside the questions of the TV correspondents, who, upon Tark's arrival, had sprung from their vans, and knocked on the Tuccis' front door.

"Mrs. Tucci?" The woman was alarmingly pregnant.

"Mhmm."

"May I come inside?"

"What is it?

"May I come inside?"

She led him to the kitchen, motioned for him to sit at their table. She sat across from him. "This is my sister Amanda," Carla Tucci said.

Tark nodded to Amanda, a pretty girl, and then looked at Carla again.

Your husband is dead, and I'm glad for it, he wanted to say. Instead: "A little while ago, down by the beach. We found a body."

And here was the strangest part: the woman, not one word. Not a tear. Not a question, not a sound. Didn't even make eye contact with her own sister. She stood and went over to the kitchen counter, and replaced the coffee filter. Scooped in some coffee grounds and began brewing a fresh pot. She stood there a moment while the machine started gurgling, then got three cups from the cabinet and set them on the table. She sat down again and faced the window. Outside, everything took on a gilded hue in the morning light. Her sister watched the floor. Nobody looked at anybody. It was as if the news hadn't even been delivered.

BEHIND THE MUSIC

L unch is two slices of pizza eaten outside the Castle of Horrors, at the picnic table overlooking the ocean. My friend Lizard is supposed to be inside working, but he's here, too, dressed as Bloody Axe Murderer, smoking a cigarette.

"Eight o'clock," he tells me. "My place. I found another drummer."

As always, Lizard's plans are last-minute. And as always, it seems, I'm available. "Who is he?"

"Teri met him at the gym."

Teri is Lizard's roommate, a massage therapist. I think she's hot, but Lizard says I'm an idiot, that she's only into old assholes with money.

"He any good?" I ask.

Lizard flicks ashes off the pier's ledge. "I fucking hope so, Casey. Said his old band had a steady night at the Bizarre Bar. He gigs a lot."

Gigging a lot means nothing. You can gig a lot and still suck, and Lizard knows it. We've been auditioning drummers for months, and it's getting maddening. I swear we're not even that choosy—we just want some talent. But in Breakneck Beach, New Jersey, finding talent isn't easy.

Angie Bailey, our boss, comes outside and squints at us.

We're all squinters, it's so dark inside the Castle of Horrors and so bright out here in July. "I need you in the Rat Tunnel," she says to Lizard. "Nobody's up there now."

"Two minutes."

Angie glares at him. "Finish the damn cigarette, and let Casey eat his lunch." She's strict with the punch-clock—she'll dock you if you're five minutes late—but when it comes to cigarette breaks, her hands are tied because all the actors smoke.

"I'll go up there," I say for about the millionth time this summer.

I'm no actor, though. Just the custodian, and only sixteen. And so Angie doesn't even bother with a response. She's heading back inside when Lizard says, "Look at that," and points down to the water. Maybe twenty feet below, a small gray bird is rolling around in the surf. A strong wave must have blindsided it. "Little sucker's toast."

Sure looks that way—though Angie must see life where I can't, because she's on the move, racing down the wooden ladder, skipping rungs and jumping the last six feet to the sand, then stomping into the water and snatching it up just as another wave crests. A minute later she's back on the pier, her sneakers and socks soaked, cutoff shorts splashed, the bird in her cupped hands. I throw the remains of my pizza into the trash, and we all surround Angie, expecting to see death. Instead, the bird's alive, sort of—an ugly fleshy thing, feathers missing, heart racing.

"It's a sandpiper," Lizard says.

"No, it's a baby seagull." She kisses its pointy head. I don't know what's gotten into her—Angie isn't the nurturing type. "Easy does it, fella. You're safe."

Lizard throws his cigarette over the railing and goes back inside the Castle to frighten people, which is his job. Angie hangs outside to watch the bird dry off on top of the cracked picnic table—where we all eat our lunches—and I go inside to throw costumes into the dryer and clean makeup out of the bathroom sink, which is my job.

An hour later, I peek outside. Angie's humming softly to the bird. Sure enough, there are little brown and white swirls, bird turds, on the tabletop. I'll be cleaning that.

"Casey," she says, "come here. I need you to watch Frederick for a minute while I get him some water."

Just like that, I'm alone with the thing. With Frederick. I feel bad for it—from trying to surf, I know what it's like being thrown around by the ocean—but I won't touch it. A bunch of feathers are missing, exposing its raw back. Looking at it makes me queasy, so I watch the waves break onto the beach and hum a song that I'm working on about being stuck in quicksand.

After work, Lizard takes me to Stuff Yer Face for calzones, then we go to his place to wait for Damian, the new drummer. I try to stay away from my parents' house as much as possible, because lately they've been royal pains. My dad stays out late completing tax returns for lazy bastards who've filed for extensions. When he comes home, he avoids Mom and me and heads straight for the TV. Sometimes I wish he had a secret life, like a second family in West Virginia or a career as a spy, because at least then there'd be something interesting about him. Instead, Dad seems happiest watching billiards on ESPN 2. Once I asked him if maybe we could find someplace to shoot pool. He looked at me as if I'd suggested we smoke crack together.

Mom's been very sad lately, which you can only tell in relation to her usual mood because she's been waking up later and going to sleep earlier, usually before Dad's shows are over for the night. She's supposedly a wedding photographer, but she hasn't booked a job in over a year. And whether it's a cause or a result of her sadness, she's gained a lot of weight this year—I'm talking fifty or sixty pounds—and that hasn't helped anything.

So Lizard's been a real savior. He's totally cool about letting me hang out, watch TV, play the guitar, whatever. We like to watch "Behind the Music" on VH1 and try and guess, before they show it, what year the featured band hit rock bottom.

At eight o'clock, Damian arrives. He's standing there at Lizard's door with a six-pack of Bud and chips and salsa like it's compensation for some atrocity he's about to commit.

"Let's rock the house," he says, and Lizard shoots me a glance. *Another one*, it says. *Another goddamn one.*

The apartment is over an office, a chiropractor who doesn't work nights, so we can make as much noise as we can stand. Teri is out tonight, working. In the apartment, there's the usual mound of clothes and used dishes and glasses all over, and there's the usual stink, like a sweaty guy's apartment, which I assume must be embarrassing for her.

"I'm pissed about the bird," I tell Lizard while we're setting up. Actually, I'm tuning my guitar while Damian's assembling his drum kit. Lizard has already tuned his bass and is picking the label off a beer.

"What? It's just a bird."

"Yeah, and who do you think's going to be cleaning up after it?"

This makes him laugh. "The professor's first job."

I hate when he calls me that. I get mostly B's in high school, and C's in math. (I got an A in English, but only after Mr. Prosser told me I was a "sloppy thinker," so I had to stick it to him.) And sure I'm going to college in a year, okay, but I'm not a brainiac by any stretch, and it just creates this wall between us when he says shit like that. Besides, it's not my first job, and he knows it. I've worked every summer since turning fourteen, and just because I still live with my parents doesn't mean I'm spoiled or precious or anything. I'm sixteen, for Christ sakes.

I give Lizard the finger, then tune the high strings.

The three of us jam on a couple original grooves. Lately, Lizard and I have been doing a Rage-Against-the-Machine-sounding thing, with the guitar and bass doubling a bluesy riff, and me shouting shit real fast into the microphone. Damian doesn't exactly suck, but he keeps itching to speed up the tempos without realizing it.

We jam for about an hour before Teri comes home. I still can't believe that Lizard, the lucky bastard, lives with this girl. She's cute with blond hair and likes to wear faded blue jeans with little horizontal rips in the ass like miniblinds so you can see her underwear.

"Hi, boys," she says, then crosses the room, emitting a scent of sweet alcohol, and immediately takes her shirt off and starts making a sandwich. She's got this pink bra on, and I'm so jealous of Lizard and Damian because somehow they just start talking to her and it's all casual. Me, I can't even look at her, though then I do and it's like I'm staring.

"I love Jaegermeister Guy," Teri sings to the room, spinning around a wooden column in the den that keeps the building standing. "You might think he's just trying to nail me, but he's not. Lizard, don't look at me like that. Don't be like that. He just doesn't enjoy drinking alone after his massage."

"How many shots did you have?" Damian asks.

"Wouldn't *you* like to know?" She laughs. "Wouldn't *I* like to know?"

I'm totally out of the conversation at this point, just trying to be cool, but I feel as if I'm alone in some other dimension, and my gaze is shooting back and forth between Teri's body and anywhere other than Teri's body, and I'm looking around at the guys and at the chips like something interesting's going on there, and I've got to say something to somebody. So I say to Lizard, "You ever see Angie act like that before?"

The conversation's natural flow comes abruptly to an end.

Lizard turns to me. "What?"

"Like she was the bird's mother."

"Bird?"

Now Damian's out of the loop, so I tell him briefly about Angie's rescue, how she doesn't seem the compassionate type. "Hell, lots of birds die in the waves, right? Part of life. So what's Angie acting like that for?"

"Casey," Lizard says, all sensitive. "Did Angie give little Casey a woody?"

There's laughter, and I say, "Fuck you."

"Don't be ashamed, my man. Angie's a babe."

He's joking. We both know she isn't. Angie herself looks like a bird, with short hair clinging to her head, a sharp nose, and skinny limbs.

"Fuck you! Here—here's some wood." There's a drumstick lying near my feet, and I throw it at him. It misses, but nails the salsa jar.

"Easy there," Teri warns, tilting her head and grinning at me. My face is on fire.

Eventually Teri says goodnight to the room, pecks Lizard on the cheek, and goes into her bedroom. But the momentum's been killed, and after a few more sloppy jams, Lizard says, "Sounds like time to call it a night."

He flicks on VH1 while Damian breaks down the kit, and I learn some interesting facts about Bonnie Tyler. Real name is Gaynor Hopkins. "Total Eclipse Of The Heart" was written by Jim Steinman. Like us, she is currently without a record deal.

I can see it coming, Lizard's foul mood, while Damian packs up. Lizard's hovering, trying to get Damian out the door quickly so that he can start brooding.

Alone with me, Lizard says, "I can't deal with these assholes anymore."

"Damian? He's okay."

We're sitting on the couch, a tan one with some buttons missing off the cushions.

"No, man. The guy can't play. I don't have time anymore for guys who can't play."

I feel a flash of pride, because indirectly he's just paid me a compliment. "Well, it's not like we're playing gigs or anything. We're just jamming."

"That's just it, man. I've got to get to the next level." He clicks off the television, then immediately clicks it on again. Then off. "Shit."

Lizard's got his bass and his job at the Castle of Horrors, but not a lot else. Music is his path to greatness, or at least to something other than forty years at the filling station where he works off-season. My future's easier: college, then Shore Public Accountants, the family business. There are big plans for me there, high expectations, because I'm not a fuck-up like some of my cousins, like Bruce, Uncle Lambert's son, who's in a juvenile detention center for beating up his assistant principal. My path isn't exciting, it isn't great, but it's clear and achievable. So music, for me, is supposed to be a hobby.

The thing is, this is complete bullshit.

It's more than a hobby. Whoever said music is like a drug sure had it right, and if nobody said that, then I'm saying it now. I'm probably the best rock guitarist in Breakneck Beach. Beats me, I just started playing four years ago, but my fingers learn things so fast, and my head can remember chords I hear, and sometimes I understand what it must feel like to be a brilliant scientist with theorems popping like corn in your head. Sometimes, now for instance, I'm jealous of Lizard for his lack of options. Choosing music, he's not giving up one damn thing.

"So what's the next level?" I ask him.

He shrugs. "I'm thinking of moving to Charlottesville once the summer's over. They've got a good scene there. Dave Matthews and all."

"Virginia? Are you serious?"

When he looks at me he's older than twenty-one. "Man," he says, "I could spin my wheels here forever. I got to make contacts. Breakneck Beach is a joke, and Charlottesville's as good as anyplace."

"But I thought we had something here." It's a dumb thing to say. We have nothing, and I don't know why I'm panicking and being all possessive. "You don't know anyone in Charlottesville, do you? It'd be starting all over. You want that? Do you have any idea how hard that will be?"

"Hey, buddy," he says. "Don't count yourself out. Maybe you'll catch up with me in a year or two. Blow off college for a while, come down to Charlottesville, and we'll tour the Southeast."

"Yeah. Sure."

"Or maybe," he says, smirking, "I'll be too good for you by then."

To my surprise, when I get home at eleven-thirty, Mom's still awake, sitting at the kitchen reading *Cosmopolitan*. A small plate with crumbs and an open can of Dr. Pepper are on the table, and what I want to ask her is why she doesn't at least *try* diet soda.

"Hey," I say.

When she sees me, she closes the magazine quickly, and I feel as though I've caught her at something. She puts the magazine on the table.

Now I notice that her eyes are bloodshot and puffy like she's been crying. "What?" I ask and sit down next to her. I assume she's been looking at the models, which doesn't do anyone any good.

She takes my hand. Hers is pale and soft. "Your father. He has a girlfriend. I threw him out."

The words are far more dramatic than any I'd have imagined ever coming out of my mother's mouth, in our boring house, and for a moment it doesn't compute. My dad is the slug on the couch. He doesn't understand jokes. He doesn't love music or talk about interesting things. And he barely has time for Mom, let alone for some other woman, because he's always at the office.

Ah.

I should be angry with him. Furious. Or I should be sad, realizing how fragile our family is. I want to sympathize immediately with my mother. But Dad has a secret life after all, and I almost feel proud of the bastard for breaking free of my own withered expectations of him. Instead of feeling what I know I should be feeling, all I wonder is what that girlfriend looks like. If she's pretty.

The thing I say is: "Wow," and then we both just sit there, holding hands and looking off in different directions for maybe five minutes, sighing occasionally, until the phone rings. It's my dad, I can tell right away by my mother's flat tone. I go to my bedroom to stare at the ceiling until I fall asleep with the lights on, hoping to dream about Teri and her ripped jeans, though I don't.

When I awaken at four a.m. and my bedroom light is still on, I feel a childish disappointment that despite her own problems, my mother hasn't stopped in to kill the light before going to bed.

Happy Land's midway is crowded this morning. They're predicting thunderstorms later, but now it's as bright as summer gets. I go inside the Castle of Horror's backstage area, and as soon as I punch in, Angie corners me.

"You know where Lizard's at?"

"No," I answer, and think, the bastard's done it, he's gone

to Charlottesville. Just when my parents are splitting up, just when I know I'm going to need some serious distraction. I spend the next hour torn between hating him for leaving without saying goodbye, and burning with jealousy. I imagine him in his Camaro, windows down, blasting the radio, pumping the horn at cute chicks, the grit on his Michelins his last connection to Breakneck Beach. He's already forgotten my name. By tonight, he'll find the city's key music shop and ask where to find the best players in town. I'll be home with Mom watching BRAVO, or, worse, with Dad at the diner while he muddles through some lame prepared speech—why he's left us for some (probably ugly) other woman, how he's still my father, blah, blah.

Later that morning, Angie is outside at the picnic table feeding Frederick, and I'm out there hauling bags of trash, when Lizard shows up with a Dunkin' donut and no excuse except laziness.

"Consider yourself on notice," Angie tells him without even looking up. "I got a dozen people who'd kill for your job."

Lizard salutes, actually clicks his heels together, and says, "Ma'am, yes, Ma'am," which can't go over well.

"You're on Wolfman today," she says. It's cruel punishment—the Wolfman costume is bulky, hot, and smells like sausage.

When Lizard walks away, he gives me a wink. He looks too happy. I don't like it and follow him inside.

"What gives?" I ask.

Lizard is an enormous mouthful of donut. Flakes are falling to the floor that I'll have to clean later. He waits a second, chewing, building suspense, until I'm frothing to know.

"Me and Teri," he says finally. "Last night, it all came together. Turns out she loves me. Can you believe it? I fucking love that girl, too."

Bullshit. "Dude, you don't love Teri. You never even talk about her."

"Yeah? Well, I fucking love her."

This makes less than zero sense. Yesterday he was all but packed to leave. To make contacts. To begin life as a professional musician. And sure, I wanted Lizard around because we were friends and bandmates. And yes, minutes ago I was pissed at him for leaving. But not as pissed at him as I am now for staying. Because breaking free of Breakneck Beach, I've decided, is exactly what Lizard ought to do—even if it means me losing my friend and bassist—and he's being chicken-shit.

"What about Charlottesville?" I ask. "What about your career?"

"What about it? I'm talking love here. It changes everything." He actually whistles. "Imagine—love, right in my own goddamn apartment. Right under my goddamn nose."

The rain begins at three o'clock and crescendos into a mad drum roll on the Castle's roof. The park empties out, and at four o'clock we're allowed to leave early. Lizard asks me if I want to hang at his place until Teri comes home, but I say no. He takes me home, and I'm bad company in the car because I'm still pissed at him. Been pissed all day long, so much so that I don't even tell him that my parents are splitting up. Lizard and Teri can get married and spend the next fifty years together, for all I care, have twenty beautiful children and five hundred grandchildren, all with beautiful asses like their grandmother, and they can all get together for family fucking reunions and have sack races till Tuesday, and I'll still say Lizard's a coward. It isn't love.

When we pull up to the house, I almost tell Lizard about my parents, but again I don't. I want that over him, knowing something important and keeping it to myself.

"Call me tonight," he says. "We need to talk drummers."

Inside, Mom is at Dad's computer, in his office, typing. All Dad's papers, bank statements, and accounting journals that normally cover everything are stacked neatly by the wall. Mom's hair is down, it's messy, and she's got on blue jeans and a button-down shirt I've never see before, like you'd wear to an office. She looks like somebody busy at something, which is a refreshing look for her.

"What're you doing?" I ask. Letters to lawyers, I assume.

"I'm writing a novel."

This is such an out-of-the-blue answer that I wish someone else, a notary, were here to verify it.

"What?"

"I'm going to try being a novelist." She cracks her knuckles. "It's something I've always wanted to try."

She's never mentioned it before. I've never seen her write anything except grocery lists. Yet the monitor is filled with text. The word *bustier* jumps off the screen at me.

"What about being a wedding photographer?" I ask.

"What about it?"

I'm still looking at the monitor. *Ravaging. Cowboy hands.* "Why don't you try being that?"

She puts her hands back on the keyboard. "Get out, Casey."

At this point, I ride my bike back toward the Castle. The rain has softened, until I'm halfway there when it picks up again even stronger than before. There's thunder, too, huge crashes, and it's one of those seashore thunderstorms that's both frightening and dazzling. I get beyond drenched and nearly fall off the bike twice. When I arrive, Happy Land is still open, technically, though the rain's driven everyone away, and only a skeleton staff roams the midway.

At the Castle, Angie's in the sound room watching her bird hop across the console. It goes right over to the wall and starts pecking at the outlet, and Annie guides it away with her hand.

Though she's management now, legend is that Angie used to be the scariest damn actor in the whole place. The actors talk about her when she isn't around, and everyone's got a theory: that her parents locked her in a shack; that she never went to school; that she killed her parents in Nevada because they beat her so bad; that underneath her shirt is a maze of scars; that she was raised in a religious compound in Florida; that she raised herself since the age of twelve. Ten. Eight.

I've seen her eyes and know that some of it must be true. Not exactly her eyes—maybe the lines around her eyes. Maybe it's her mouth. But now, here, Angie's body is a perfect image of contentment

She looks up at me. "Casey, what are you doing here?"

I'm there to look at her, I think. "How's Frederick?"

"God, you're soaked." She gets up and comes to me. "Did you leave something here?"

I want to ask how old she is. Instead, I say, "How is he?"

"He's a bird," she says. "Come with me." She leads me to the costume rack. Everyone's gone for the day, and plenty of clean costumes are hanging on the rack. She unhooks the Crazy Soldier costume and hands it to me. "Put this on. Dry your clothes."

I go into the bathroom and put on the bloody fatigues, then put my wet clothes into the dryer and turn it on. She's back inside the sound room, so I go in there. I wonder if Angie's a babe or not. She looks nothing like Teri, who's all curves and brightness. Angie is sharp angles—elbows and wrists and a pointy chin. No, she isn't a babe. Still, I think about kissing her, just walking over there and putting my lips on hers. Even if she's twenty-five. Even if she's thirty. I think about it, but I know I'm not going to do it.

"You look good in that," she says.

In this situation, good means bad. Frightening. "Then

let me scare people," I say. She's about to say no again, I can feel it. "Come on, Angie, the park's closing in an hour."

"There's no one left to scare," she says. "The park's cleared out."

"I don't care." I want to be in there, where a Crazy Soldier belongs. Where the Crazy Soldier runs the whole goddamn show. "Let me anyway. Not everyone's gone home."

She bites her pinky nail. "Pick me out a costume. We'll both go."

I head back to the bathroom and add to my own costume the armbands, the boots, then put on some camouflage makeup we keep above the sink.

For Angie, I choose the Lizzie Borden, because it's skimpy and there's a chance she'll change into it right there in the sound room. And she does. She turns away from me but knows I'm watching. Her back, I learn, isn't a maze of scars. Rather, it's pale and smooth, and her spine is straight and pronounced, and she wears a purple bra and white panties that seem too big on her, and I find that I like knowing these things about her, things that are secret from Lizard and the other actors and everyone on this planet, maybe, but Angie and me. Seeing her ordinary spine, her plain underwear, I suspect that Angie isn't from Florida or Nevada, but rather from Long Branch or Shrewsbury, somewhere not far, not special.

And this belief—the possibility that Angie isn't special, this woman with me on a stormy Thursday afternoon— shoots electricity right through me, teeth to toe. I don't know then that as we stand there, Happy Land is going broke, and that the Castle of Horrors will burn down in just a few weeks, conveniently—suspiciously—the morning after Labor Day, when the park is closed and nobody is inside. What happens to Angie after that, I won't know. But today, this Thursday afternoon in the Wolfman's Den, I'll brush up against Angie until it isn't subtle anymore, and she'll straddle me amid the papier-mâché boulders, the rubber rats, and a looping Bernard Herrmann soundtrack. It won't be the only time, either. Until the season ends, we'll make a point to find ourselves together in the long shadows of the Torture Chamber, the Cemetery, the Wicked War Zone, Frankenstein's Laboratory, and on and on.

Now, when we exit the sound room, Angie says, "Be good, Frederick," as if saying goodnight to a child, but she doesn't close the door behind us. I wonder briefly if that's smart, leaving the bird to get lost or electrocuted or squashed.

"Angie," I begin, "I'm worried—"

"Take it easy," she says. "Just be quiet and follow me." We walk past the dryer, which is humming warmly, to the flimsy door that separates us from them, and then go through it.

WE THE PEOPLE

T ommy, my enemy, volunteers to hand back the quizzes. When he walks up my row, I trip him. First, though, I make sure Mrs. Pridget isn't looking—she's waddled over to the windows and is opening them because it's ninety degrees in here. Tommy lands on his knees and drops the quizzes, which swoosh across the floor. Everyone laughs and then stops laughing when Mrs. Pridget turns around and says, "Hush!" Her eyes scan the class. "I'll give every one of you detention in half a heartbeat."

She will, too. I've known since the third grade that Mrs. Pridget is the meanest teacher in the school. She's mean and has a humpback, and she wears gobs of blue makeup around her eyes so that you don't look at the hump. You can't start Brendan Byrne Elementary School and not hear about Mrs. Pridget. She'll call your parents without thinking twice. Said so, right on the first day: "I always keep your parents involved, whether they want to be or not." And I do *not* want my parents involved. You have no idea what Pop is like. He's the strongest man in the county.

I'm the class bully (every class has got one, and I'm it) and the biggest kid in the class—biggest because I got left back once—so she'll want to make me an example. I learned that about Mrs. Pridget in third grade, too. That each year she picks out a boy, somebody she can really torture, and makes him cry like a girl. This summer, I begged Mom to transfer me into Mr. Kowalsky's class. She tried, but his class was full.

Tommy finishes returning the quizzes, then plops down again at the first desk in the third row. He's wearing his shirt untucked for once. His hair still is parted on the side like an old man's, but it doesn't look as neat as usual. Like his mommy didn't dress him today. I whisper, "Do you want your mommy, Tommy?" He doesn't move a muscle, so I know he's heard me.

Tommy's mom is the Art Lady every year. Once a month she comes to class and shows us art. His mom is nice and smells like the mall. She tells us about the paintings and brings chocolate chip cookies made from scratch. Best cookies ever. I don't see how she can be related to Tommy. He's a brat. He talks too much, and he volunteers for everything like returning quizzes and staying inside during lunch to change the bulletin boards. He *makes* teachers like him. But his mom's chocolate chip cookies are soft, and—

Wait. Wait.

Mrs. Pridget is looking right at me. Wait. Now she's not. I'm scribbling on the back of my notebook. I do it all the time. Someday she's going to catch me and yell. But I can't help scribbling. I draw good pictures of tanks and bombs and planets exploding in other solar systems. And I can draw the Incredible Hulk. I like how when David Banner becomes the Hulk, he turns green and his clothes rip because he's growing huge muscles and he has the strength of ten men and he can run as fast as cars.

If you make me angry, I'll turn into the Hulk. When this happens, when I'm the Hulk, I have superhuman strength, but I can't control myself. I *have* to beat up whoever made me angry. Unless it's a teacher. Even when I'm the Hulk I know I can't beat up a teacher. So it makes me frustrated and sometimes I cry. But if a kid makes fun of me for crying, I'll beat him up later. Been suspended twice for beating kids up. The second time, Pop came to the principal's office to get me. "Mark my word," I remember him saying to the principal, "this ain't happening again."

The walk from Mr. Melnick's office to Pop's car was the scariest walk ever. By then I wasn't the Hulk anymore, just me again, bracing myself. Walking across the parking lot, I pretended to look down at my shoes but really I was looking out of the corner of my eyes at Pop. Pop's into the sneak-attack, though, and it wasn't until back home, hours later, that I woke up (I'd fallen asleep watching TV) being dragged onto the floor by my hair while Mom shrieked from too far across the house to be of any help.

Mrs. Pridget asked the class a question, I think. I was drawing a rocket ship about to blast off (there are giant smoke bubbles at the bottom of the launch pad), but I think she asked a question. Now Tommy's waving his hand in the air, but Mrs. Pridget won't call on him. She's looking around for somebody else. That's funny, because Tommy always gets called on when he wants. Finally, she says, "Tommy, will you stop waving your hand around like a helicopter?" and kids laugh at him again but then stop laughing after a second because they don't want to get in trouble, and Tommy lowers his hand slowly like it's the opposite of a snake being charmed by a snake charmer.

The Preamble to the Constitution is fifty-two words long. It begins, "We the people," and then has lots of other words that don't make any sense. We have to memorize all of them and say them back out loud, in front of the whole class, without making any mistakes. I mean *any* mistakes. We can't even say, "Um." We have one night to learn it. Then each of us will stand up and say it out loud and try not to mess up. If you mess it up you get one more chance. If you mess it up a second time, you get an F.

On the walk home from school, I always stop at the Wawa and buy a Yoo-hoo and a three-pack of Ring Dings. I'm ten years old, so I can stay home by myself after school. Mom comes home at five-thirty usually. Sometimes she comes home later. She's a secretary at an important company. When I get home today, Pop's van is outside, and when I go inside I can hear the television. Mom drops me off at Pop's apartment on Saturdays, so it's weird seeing him now, here, in Mom's den. He's leaning back on the couch, legs up on the glass coffee table. Mom yells at me for doing that. The channel changer is on his belly. He has his painting clothes on.

He turns his head to me and nods. "Son. Beer."

I go to the refrigerator and look, but there aren't any beers, so I get him a can of Diet Coke and then sit next to him on the couch. He's watching The People's Court. There's a woman complaining and waving her arms. Pop mutes the television but keeps looking at it. "Tell me what my son's been up to."

"We have to memorize the Preamble to the Constitution," I say.

"Hmm." He shrugs. "Well, memorize it, then. You're a bright boy." He raises the can to his lips and notices it's not beer. He takes a long swallow anyway and puts the can down on the coffee table. Pop's knuckles are crusted with white paint and look like the top of a mountain range. Splotches of dried paint cover Pop's painting clothes. Last Halloween, I wanted to dress up as a painter and wear Pop's painting shirt and walk around carrying one of his rollers. But he got angry, said I couldn't, no way, that he didn't ever want me wearing his painter's clothes. So Mom bought me a plastic Ninja mask that made my face sweat. By then, I didn't feel like going trick-or-treating, but I went anyway because I sort of still did.

"Why're you here?" I ask, because I'm curious what Pop's doing in Mom's house.

He says, "What time's your mother getting home?"

"Five-thirty," I say, hoping it's the truth. Pop doesn't need to know that last night she stayed out until ten o'clock. I can make myself dinner, and he doesn't need to get mad at Mom. He's called the past couple nights asking for her, and I've had to cover, saying she was in the shower or at the Wawa buying orange juice.

"We'll see about that," Pop says, and then we both look at the television for a few minutes. Fridays at nine, we used to sit like this together and watch *The Incredible Hulk*. It scared me at first, until Pop showed me how, each episode, David Banner always became angry and changed into the Hulk exactly twice, at exactly the same times: twenty minutes into the show, and again just before it ended. Once I could predict David Banner's anger, it wasn't so bad.

But I don't know how to watch television with Pop anymore. It feels tense, now, like maybe he'll say I'm a good boy but maybe he'll smack me in the ear. I say, "I'm going to try memorizing that stuff." He nods, and I take my social studies book out of my knapsack and go down the hall to my bedroom. As I swing my bedroom door shut, I can hear the television's sound come on again.

I sit at my desk, open the social studies book to the Preamble to the Constitution, and try to remember the words. But it's impossible. How do you even begin? I think of Tommy Hilliard and wonder how *he's* learning the Preamble. I picture him at the kitchen table with a plate of cookies and a stack of flashcards that his mother wrote out for him. I'll bet she's memorizing the words right along with him, speaking them in that soft voice she uses to explain the paintings she brings to class. I go over to my bed and lie down with the book. There are too many words, and they are long and impossible to understand, and even if I could lie here and work on remembering each one, I might lose track of time, and that's the last thing I want—because more than anything I'm afraid of five-thirty coming and Mom not being home and Pop waiting and waiting and getting angrier. So I look at the words that I can't memorize, stare at them on page fifteen of my social studies book called *New Frontiers*, and I'm worrying so much that it's unbelievable to me how I could fall asleep.

I wake to them fighting.

Pop's voice is louder than Mom's. It's nearly dark through my window, and I don't know whether it's night or day, and for a few seconds, I forget they've split up. Then I remember when it is and where I am. I lean over and look at the clock radio. Seven-thirty, but it feels later. I'm hungry.

I lie still, trying not to make the bed creak, so that I can make out as many words as possible. Pop says things like "running wild" and "irresponsible," and I wish he didn't think these things about me. I fight with kids, yeah, but I don't run wild. On Mischief Night, the night before Halloween, Mom didn't even let me outside to throw eggs. And anyway, he should be yelling at me, not Mom. I can tell, too, that he's mad at Mom for coming home late. Mom has to work at night sometimes, I wish I could explain to Pop, but I don't mind so much. If I go in there and make even one peep right now, though, I'll get clobbered. I wish I could hear more, but the television is still on out there, and they're not talking loud enough for me to hear everything. Mom sounds like she's hissing at Pop, hissing like a cat or a snake, and I want to cry, but I won't.

Then I hear Pop's footsteps coming fast toward my door. I pretend to be asleep. He shoves the door open hard enough for the knob to make a dent in the wall. My eyes open, and when I see him I know it's trouble. His face is red like he's had lots of beer, only I know he hasn't. "Come out here," he says, and then heads back toward the kitchen. When I get there, Pop is seated at the table and Mom is pacing the area near the microwave with a cup of coffee in her hand. She has on a yellow shirt and a skirt with little patterns on it like seashells. Her hair is pinned back like it always is when she comes home from work. She's been crying, I can tell.

"The boy's got to memorize the Preamble," my pop says, like he's accusing Mom of something. I know he's being tricky with his words, that my mom doesn't know what "the Preamble" means, but she's not about to ask and let my pop seem smarter than she is. She sips from her coffee and looks to me for help.

I say, "We have to memorize—"

Pop cuts me off: "If you were here," he says to Mom, "you'd know."

"*I'd know?*" she says. "Let me tell you, I know plenty. Oh, there's plenty I know. . . ." But she's done. She's tired, and the fight isn't in her. She rubs her eyes with her fingertips. I wish she and I were here alone to eat dinner.

"Howard," Pop says, "pack some clothes and your toothbrush. And your homework." He slaps the tabletop hard with his thick palm. "*Move.*"

So I move.

We sit in the smoking section of the Four Seasons Diner, and he smokes two cigarettes before we order cheddar burgers. He's puckering his lips around the cigarettes and making a sick sucking sound. Inside the diner, the smoke makes my nose hurt and my Coke taste funny.

Pop's in some kind of trance, not talking to me but breathing slowly through the cigarette, and I know to sit there and not talk. I drink some of my water, but even that I do as quietly as possible. Then I read my placemat, which talks about different state parks in New Jersey. Most of the names are long and sound like Indian tribes when I mouth them to myself.

Pop puts out his second cigarette in a glass ashtray that has other people's dirty ashes in it. "Let's look at that Preamble, son," he says, and I pull the social studies book out of my knapsack and show it to him.

"Hmm," he says. "Okay, start."

But I haven't tried to learn it yet. "We the people," I say.

"Okay."

"That's all I know."

"Shit." He lays the book flat on the table, covering his bread plate. "We the people of the United States. Say it."

I do. "In order to form," he says. "Say it."

"In order to form."

"Now all of it."

"We the people," I say, and I'm stuck. I'm an idiot who can't remember anything. The space behind my eyes starts to tingle, and I know I'm going to cry. We try some more, but by the time the burgers come I've barely gotten the first eleven words.

After two bites, I can tell that my burger is well-done, burned almost, though I said medium rare. We're eating and not saying anything to each other when all of a sudden Pop takes a long drink of his beer. He bangs the mug down, takes a deep breath, and then lets it out in a long sigh, his arms outstretched like he's just won a race. "This ain't so bad, is it?"

I'm alone with Pop in this smoky, smelly diner, and I know it's hopeless and that I'm never going to be able to recite all fifty-two words tomorrow without messing up even once, and the waitress, sitting on a counter stool picking at her stocking, reminds me of Mom—she's sitting like Mom sits with one foot crossed up high over the other leg—and I look over at the mirror on the wall and see through its reflection that it's smokier than I thought in here, and Pop's in his painter's clothes, and I'm sitting there opposite him with my disgusting burger, and we're looking like we're both a hundred years old.

With my mouth full of burger, I start crying. When I inhale, I feel myself start to choke, so I spit out the chewed-up burger onto my plate.

"Howard?" he says. "Son?"

I keep coughing even though I spat out my burger. I'm coughing and crying, and since the diner is empty it's echoing in there, and I know the waitress is watching me even though I don't check. I grab for the water and drink some and am able to calm myself down enough to breathe regularly.

"Christ, Howard, what is it?" Pop asks. "What?"

I want to tell him that it's *this*, this moment that's the matter. Being here. At this diner. Pop and me. But I realize this is something I can't say to him because it's just mean, and he won't understand, and besides, being here together is exactly what Pop wants most.

I tell him that I forgot to pack toothpaste.

We're at the diner from eight-thirty until eleven o'clock. When we finally leave, I'm freezing cold and so tired that I start to cry again, only this time it's quieter, like I'm whimpering, and I feel like a baby. "Stop that nonsense, Howard," Pop says. "Just stop it or I'll smack you." After he pays the check, he makes me say the entire Preamble to the waitress. I get all the way through it, except I say "um" a couple times, and I know that's what's going to kill me tomorrow. The waitress claps for me politely, and Pop says, "Ha!" Even though I'm a trick dog and still sniffling, it feels pretty good.

I don't stay at Pop's apartment that night. He's got to work early in the morning and says it's easier for me to get to school from Mom's. He calls the house from the diner and says he's dropping me off.

I fall asleep in the van and wake up when we hit the bump pulling into the driveway. Mom meets us at the front door. Her hair is down, makeup off, and she's dressed in a

Cape May t-shirt that comes down to her knees. She kisses me on the ear and says I should go straight to bed, which is all I want anyway. Pop squeezes me on the shoulder so hard that I have to squirm away. He says, "Goodnight, son," to me but doesn't say a single word to Mom before turning around and walking to his car.

In the morning, Mom makes me a breakfast that's so big I can't eat half of it. I smelled it the minute I woke up. Now, in the kitchen, instead of cereal and milk, it's fluffy eggs and pancakes and Bob Evans sausage patties.

"I'm sorry I've been coming home so late," Mom says. Whenever Mom's sorry, she makes me eat a lot.

I stir the sausage around the syrup with my fork. "It's okay."

"No, it isn't. Tonight, your mother will be home by five. Maybe four-thirty." She comes over with the pan and spoons more egg onto my plate. Over her dress, Mom's wearing an apron that says, *All this and she cooks.* "And by then, your homework had better be done, buster." She winks at me, but she isn't a good winker and the other eye sort of closes, too. "We'll have a fun dinner tonight. You and me."

"Pizza?" I ask, hoping.

"I thought we'd make hamburgers," she says.

I set my fork down on the table too hard, and it bounces onto my lap. I try not to let my vision get swimmy. "That's what I had *last* night with Pop."

"Careful with the silverware. Don't get moody, Howard." Mom removes the apron, folds it, and puts it in the drawer under the sink. "We won't have hamburgers if you don't want."

"I want pizza. You said we could have something fun. You *said* so—"

"Okay, okay." She comes over and kisses me on the head, then sits down opposite me at the table. She sighs. "It's just that I have ground beef already in the freezer. That's all I was thinking. I can put onion powder into the beef. And oregano. It wouldn't be anything like last night."

"I want *pizza*. That's the only thing I want." I don't even know whether that's true. I'm so full of eggs right now that my gut hurts.

Mom purses her lips. "Let's not start the day so moody."

Tommy Hilliard has on the same clothes as yesterday.

I suppose I watch Tommy a lot during the day because there isn't much else to do while Mrs. Pridget is talking. He's wearing a green and yellow striped shirt and brown corduroy pants—the same, I'm positive, as yesterday. "Nice shirt, Tommy," I whisper when Mrs. Pridget is shutting the door and can't hear me. Normally he wouldn't say anything, because I'd kill him. So I'm surprised when he spins around in his chair and says, "Shut it, Howard!"

Tommy's eyes have bags under them, like in cartoons, and his hair is so messed up you can barely tell it's supposed to have a side part. His shirt is all wrinkled from yesterday. My mom would never send me to school with the same clothes two days in a row. Even when she spent three nights in the motel (before Pop moved to his apartment), she came home early in the morning to make sure I was ready for school. I can't picture Tommy's mom, the Art Lady, letting Tommy come to school like this. But she has.

An amazing thing happens then. Mrs. Pridget nails *Tommy*, not me. "Turn around, Tommy, and mind your own business," she says.

I'm stunned. No teacher has ever yelled at Tommy before. He faces front, puts his elbows on the desk, and rests his chin on his palms. All through attendance and morning announcements he sits like that, not moving an inch. After the Pledge of Allegiance, Mrs. Pridget says it's time to begin reciting the Preamble. She's going to start at the beginning of the alphabet and work her way through. My last name's Spencer, so I've got a while to wait.

Tracy Adams goes first. Mrs. Pridget makes her stand. Tracy sounds nervous, but she speaks slowly and gets it on her first try. I hate her. She's not even that smart but she gets it perfect. When she finishes, Mrs. Pridget makes some mark in her grade book and says, "Very good, Tracy." Her voice makes me think of spoiled fruit.

The next three people (Cokie, Raymond and Glenn) mess it up on the first try but they get it on the second, though I'm sure I heard Glenn say "Uh" once. But he got credit anyway, he's so lucky.

All this time I'm mouthing the words to myself along with whoever's speaking, and I begin to realize that I know it. There's "We" and "the" and "people," and though ahead of whatever word I'm mouthing is like a dark cave where I can't see, when I get there, I find the next word waiting for me. There's "establish" and "justice" and "domestic" and "tranquility." They just come, one after the other after the other. There's "liberty" and "do" and "ordain." I think I know it better than anyone, because they all seem to struggle for maybe a word or two, but not me.

I'm thinking how amazing it'll be tonight, calling Pop and telling him that I didn't mess up even once, not a single "um," when Mrs. Pridget says: "Tommy Hilliard."

Tommy stands but doesn't say anything.

"You may begin, Tommy," she says.

There's silence for another few seconds. Tommy stands there but doesn't say anything. Finally, though I can barely hear his voice, he says, "Mrs. Pridget, can I talk to you?"

That's something I'd never think to do. It's almost like Tommy's an adult. He's going to tell Mrs. Pridget in private what happened to him yesterday, or this morning, so that she'll maybe let him try the Preamble again tomorrow.

"Tommy," Mrs. Pridget's says, "you may talk to me *after* your turn. Now begin."

Everyone's watching and now knows there's a big problem with Tommy. The room's quiet enough to hear people's clothes. Somewhere down the hall, a janitor's wheeling his supplies.

Tommy says, "Mrs. Pridget…," but that's all he can think to say. It's like he's reminding her of something she already knows, only she won't listen.

"Begin," she says. "Begin, Tommy."

"We," he says. "The. People." He stops. "In." He can tell from Mrs. Pridget's face—the ugliest smile of all time—that he's messed up, but she lets him dangle there a while before saying, "No. That's wrong. Now start over." She scans the room. "This is what happens when you don't study, children."

But she isn't talking to anybody other than Tommy. Around the room, kids are sitting stiff in the chairs, silent, eyes wide—same as mine—as if we're all watching television. Tommy sounds like he's watching something different, a funny movie, and laughing so hard he can't stop. Then I realize he's sobbing. Blubbering like a baby, loud. When he turns to the side, I see that his face is wet and snotty. "I don't know," he says, and groans.

"Begin." Mrs. Pridget's eyes are wide, too. She's excited. She wants him to mess up. She's trying to teach us something, I guess, but I don't understand why she's torturing Tommy. And I can't figure out why it's making me want to whisper the words to him. I won't, though, because then *I'll* get in trouble. "*Begin*," she repeats.

"I—don't—know!" Tommy blurts out.

"Don't you yell at me!" Mrs. Pridget squashes her lips together but her jaws keep moving like she's got live fish in there trying to get out. She puts her hands on her fat hips. "Don't you *ever* yell at me." She's being tricky. It isn't about his not knowing the Preamble anymore. Now it's about his yelling at her. That's a tricky thing she just did, and I come even closer to whispering, *We the people of the United States....*

Tommy's sort of swaying. He can barely keep standing, so he starts to sit down.

"Get up," Mrs. Pridget says. "You're going to remain standing until you try again. Now begin. *Begin.*"

He can't do it. He doesn't know the words. Tommy tries to keep standing, but now he's wobbling and lets out another groan, a quieter one, like it comes a long way from inside himself. And it's then I realize what Tommy needs more than anything, more than reciting the Preamble or being left alone, even. He needs to change into the Incredible Hulk. But he can't do that, either. I've been in class with Tommy since the third grade. He'll stand there for days, crying and wishing, and even if something bad *has* happened, so bad that his mom the Art Lady didn't help him memorize the Preamble, that she let him come to school in the same shirt and the same pants and maybe even the same underpants, Tommy Hilliard will not become the Hulk. The Hulk isn't in him.

I'm the Hulk, though. I can already hear that familiar sound in my head, the one that marks the start of the transformation, a sound like toilet-water rising after you flush, and I feel my eyes turning green and my muscles starting to grow. I feel my shirt getting tighter, tighter, and soon it's going to burst. I'm a force of nature, a big green tree. Only this time, it's different. I'm not just throwing a kickball at your face or pushing you over while you tie your shoe. This time, I'm the real Incredible Hulk, the monster who fights good, just battles and ends up walking alone to the saddest music you ever heard.

The kids are watching me now, not Tommy. Me. They're sliding away in their chairs, afraid of my anger and where it might get unleashed. Mrs. Pridget, too, is watching me, her eyes wider than ever but with an expression I haven't seen before, her teeth showing, her face full of lines. And I'm watching me, too. I see myself rise from my chair and stand eight feet tall. *Howard,* Mrs. Pridget says. *Howard!* But I've got green-lava blood pumping through me now and am already running to the front of the room, already swinging. In ten seconds I'm a goner. But until then I am the Hulk, Mrs. Pridget is backing away, and this classroom—this world—is mine.

POPULATION 204

No customers were in the Wawa food mart when the thunderclap hit and the lights went out. At one a.m. there were just the three of us—me in the stockroom tagging cans, Jillian on the register, and Phillip behind the hoagie counter. I felt my way out of the stockroom and looked around the store. The emergency lights had come on and were casting long, weird shadows. And while normally the place is filled with buzzing and humming from the refrigeration unit, the cash register, the air-conditioning— now, nothing. Just the rain hitting the roof overhead and the pavement outside. Jillian and Phillip were looking at me for advice or maybe reassurance. I wasn't used to being looked at for those things. I wasn't even their boss. But after the manager and the assistant manager, I was next in the chain of command. So I told them, "Maybe it'll come back on real quick."

It didn't. We listened to the rain and waited. The rain got heavier, then heavier still. A few people went by on the sidewalk, hunched into themselves underneath their raincoats and umbrellas. Usually this time of night our customers were quiet, middle-aged guys like myself looking for milk and TV dinners. Or they're teenagers with the munchies. Business was slow even on clear nights, let alone a stormy one. I told Jillian and Phillip that they could go home if they wanted. It was summer in New Jersey, and without the air-conditioning the store was already getting stuffy. Customers weren't going to come in here with all the lights off, and the register wouldn't work even if they did. Phillip said thanks, but no thanks. He'd punched in already and needed the money. Standing around like this was easy work.

"You feel the same way, Jillian?" I asked.

She sniffled. "I could use the money."

"You crying?" I asked. She'd been very quiet since she got here. I mean she'd always been quiet, but tonight she was being extra quiet.

She sniffled again. "No, Joe, I'm all right." But I went to aisle three and got a box of tissues anyway.

"You should tell us what's the matter," Phillip said. "Tell us all about it." He came over and sat on Jillian's counter, on the conveyer belt that had stopped moving. I punched my thumb through the top of the tissue box to open it and handed it to Jillian. She pulled out a few tissues, set the box next to her at the register, and dried her eyes as one of the emergency lights back by the fruit flickered a few times and went out.

"So go ahead," Phillip said. "Spill your guts." Phillip studied communications at Jersey Central College, and customers seemed to like talking with him while he made their hoagies. He was very outgoing for a guy with so many pimples on his face. Jillian, on the other hand, kept to herself, rarely saying more to the customers than *Enjoy your day*, or more to Phillip than *Good morning* or *Is there cheese on this hoagie?* So Phillip must have been hoping that with the lights off and him sitting so close, Jillian might open up a little.

"I received a letter today," she said. "My grandmother fell and broke her hip."

"Well, that's too bad," I said. "She an old lady, your grandmother?"

"Eighty-three."

"That's too bad for her—when you break your hip at that age, isn't much chance you're going to walk again." I wasn't saying it to be mean, just stating a fact of life.

"How'd she fall?" Phillip asked. "Stairs?"

"She fell off a tightrope," Jillian said. Phillip looked at me, but I didn't know what to say to that.

Jillian came out from behind the register and opened up a beach chair with porpoises on it that we sold for $9.99. She set the box of tissues on the floor next to her and sighed. "When you drive to my hometown, there's a sign at the border saying Population 204." Phillip was looking at her skeptically. So was I. I'd never heard of a town that small. "This is in Missouri," she said. "A pretty little town in the Ozark Mountains."

So here was her life story, I thought. Unlike Phillip, I wasn't so determined to get quiet people to start talking. I figured that not talking was their right. I felt like not talking myself sometimes, and while Phillip wasn't a bad kid, I had no special urge to communicate with him. Sure, I was lonely, I could have told him. Hadn't seen a naked woman outside of a magazine for four years, not since Lilah's speech got muddy and her memories went haywire and the population of my apartment decreased by one. I could have told him about that. But I wasn't going to.

Jillian must have felt different from me, though, because here came her life story, just for the asking—even if the part about her grandmother walking a tightrope at eighty-three made no sense at all. And when she went on to say that everybody in her little town in the Ozarks was training to be circus performers, I knew she was pulling our leg. What I didn't know was why. I sat on the floor near the two of them, put my arms around my knees, and listened to

Jillian talk about the town's children learning to guess people's weight and juggle flaming torches and ride unicycles and paint their faces. "And my best friend growing up," she said, "was a lion named Grouchy."

That old lion was a regular piece of work from the sound of it, rolling around on its back so that you'd scratch its belly and always on the lookout for apple butter. But that wasn't all. This town of hers had a tightrope—the one that led to her grandmother's busted hip—tied between an old sugar maple tree and the schoolhouse. Every day at lunchtime the children in town had to walk the length of the rope before heading home to eat their sandwiches.

"Sounds pretty difficult," I said.

"It wasn't so hard," she said. "Though some days we'd be blindfolded. Other days, we'd have to walk backwards. Anyone fell and the whole class had to start again." Each spring, she explained, the town put on a festival for all the neighboring towns, two whole weeks of circus acts, and part of it was showing off all of the children's new skills.

I wasn't too comfortable sitting on the ground, but I wasn't about to move. This was by far the most I'd heard out of Jillian since she'd applied for the job two years earlier.

"The problem," she said, "was that the town's population was 204. Like the sign said. You've seen signs like that, haven't you? When you drive into a town?"

"I've seen it," I said. "Never a town that small, though."

"Well, in Missouri, towns can get even smaller than that. But my town had 204, like the sign said. Whenever someone died, somebody new was needed in town so that the population would stay at 204. After a funeral, there'd be festive celebrations in the days that followed, so that people would go home and make love, and soon enough there would be a new child—"

When I laughed, Jillian narrowed her eyes as if I'd done something I shouldn't have, and I *felt* ashamed. Then her eyes widened again. "But sometimes a child would be born without someone having passed away first. Those times, people didn't like so much. It meant someone had to die."

"So that the population would stay at 204," I said soberly. She nodded.

Men coming into the Wawa were always fascinated by Jillian. They'd linger at the register and say things too goofy to say in front of their girlfriends or wives. She wasn't pretty in the usual way—her teeth were crooked, for one, and her arms were thick, and her neck had moles on it—but she had grayish blue eyes that watched you more closely than most eyes did. I would sometimes get to thinking about Jillian when I was at home alone. I didn't run into many women in the course of a day. And of the three women who worked at this Wawa, Jillian was the prettiest. I hadn't ever taken much of a liking to her personally. Not that I didn't like her. I just never felt one way or the other. But that was before I knew she would sit here with the power out and spin tales like this one, touching her throat absently with the bony fingers of her left hand, and clenching her jaw a little when recalling a detail like the brassy *oom-pah* of her mother's tuba-playing.

"Guess my weight," I said to her. "Guess it right now." Not that I even knew my own weight. Probably 230, maybe more. I'd been eating junk for a long time.

"That isn't my skill," she said. "And anyway, I'm telling a story. I'm just about to get to the important part."

But her story got interrupted by two boys, high-school age, knocking on the glass door of the Wawa. They both wore baseball caps and smirks. They looked exactly like every boy I'd ever seen in my entire life. One of them leaned his head in. "You open or what?" Water dripped from the brim of his cap onto the floor.

"Look like we're open?" I didn't get up.

"We're dying for some Wa-dogs, man. Come on, we're starving."

Stoned, too. At night, kids coming in here were always drunk or stoned. I knew they didn't mean it as a personal insult, but I couldn't help thinking of it that way. As if we were people you couldn't come and visit sober.

"We're closed," I said.

After the kids had left, I said to Jillian and Phillip that we ought to eat some hotdogs. Over by the hoagie counter was a machine that rotated the dogs and kept them warm. But with the power off, they were just going to get cold. "What do you say?"

"Lay one on me, big guy," Phillip said. "Jillian?"

"I'm a little hungry," she said.

"Go on with your story," I said, but Jillian waited until I had gone behind the hoagie counter and gotten our dogs. I put mustard and kraut on them and carried them back. Then I went to the refrigerated section and got us each a soda. Jillian handed Phillip and me each a few tissues for napkins.

When I sat down again, we each took a bite of our hotdogs. I liked the idea of this, us all eating together. It felt like something we ought to be doing. Jillian chewed politely and then swallowed. She wiped her mouth with a tissue and explained that whenever there was a birth, one of the town's elders usually would volunteer to keep the town's population steady, but not always. "It could get thorny," she said. One day, the town needed someone to step forward and nobody would, until her favorite schoolteacher said, *I'll do it*. This teacher wasn't old; the only gray in her hair came from worrying about her students.

In a state of despair, early the next morning—and without telling anyone—Jillian did something nobody in her town had ever done: she went away, vowing never to return. All of her money bought her a used car that she drove east, farther and farther, until there were no more states to cross, no more towns. Just a studio apartment and a job as a cashier. She cut her hair short, and colored it brown, and changed her name, because she didn't want any reminders of the life she had left behind.

And after a few years, sometimes entire days went by without her thinking about life back in the Ozarks.

"But now your grandmother is ill," I said.

"Not just ill," she said. "*Old* and ill. And I just keep thinking about that sign."

"Population 204."

"That's right," she said. "So if I'm ever going to see her again—"

"Now wait just a minute," Phillip said. "How'd you find out about your grandmother's injury if nobody knows where you are?"

"My mother knows where I am," she said.

Phillip was missing the point, though, and I wanted to set him right. So what if Jillian was pulling our leg? Who cared, for that matter, why she was doing it? She was taking herself seriously, and so should we.

"Well, I sure am sorry about your situation," I said, and gave Phillip the hard look I gave him whenever he left the deli station a mess. "You must love your grandmother a lot."

"I do."

Phillip sighed. "Do you think…you'll go back there, to your circus town?" He glanced at me, and I nodded.

"I'm not sure," she said. "I'm thinking I might."

Jillian took a long draw from her soda. Phillip had already finished his, and asked Jillian for a sip. I felt like I should say something vague and uplifting. But how could I know what to say when I didn't know if her grandmother really was ill, or what sort of town she was raised in, or even if she'd ever been to Missouri? She didn't have a trace of an accent. I didn't even know if her real name was Jillian or not. I didn't know *what* to believe, or if Jillian knew for herself. But I'd have been grateful if the Wawa's lights never came on again. Later, when the sun rose and I was home again, I knew that I'd lie in bed and think about the three of us sitting together in the dark with our hotdogs and sodas. I could almost believe that we were beside a campfire, old friends telling stories from deep inside our hearts.

"I think that'd be the right thing, Jillian," I told her. "It's important to be with your family when they're sick." And before I could stop myself, I was telling them about Lilah. I didn't get emotional. I didn't need to borrow any of Jillian's tissues. But I told them things. How Lilah was exactly my height but wore heels so she'd look taller. How after she lost her sense of smell, she always overdid the perfume. I talked about headaches and seizures. I told the story of how, on one of the last good days, our car had skidded on black ice and nearly gone off a drawbridge, and how for the couple of seconds we were sliding toward the edge I had felt relieved because at least we'd go out together. And when the car had come to a stop up against the guardrail, and we knew we were alive and safe for the moment, I had felt a different sort of relief—a lot like what I was feeling right now, here in the Wawa. With the two of them. Which was probably more than I needed to say. Jillian touched her throat, and Phillip nodded, then wiped his sweaty forehead with his palm. It was getting very warm.

The rain was still hitting the roof, the sky still rumbling, and I had no reason to think the lights were coming on anytime soon. I coughed into my closed fist and suggested that we put all the fruit into shopping carts and wheel them back to the storeroom where there was a refrigerator that even without power would keep things cold for several hours.

"Right, chief," Phillip said, and hopped off the conveyer belt. He extended a hand to Jillian, helping her out of the chair.

The three of us went to the rear aisle, where the fruit was. Jillian started picking over the apples in the dark, lifting one, turning it over in her hand, setting it back down. Before long she had four small apples in her right hand and three in her left.

She threw them high in the air.

MAXIMUM SECURITY

For six weeks when I was a freshman in high school, a master musician came to our house on Friday afternoons and played the piano. It wasn't a large house, but it was a large piano—seven-foot baby grand, a pretty chestnut color. While the master musician played, I would sit on a chair next to him and watch. My father sat in his recliner, across the living room from the piano, his hands folded on his lap or holding a beer stein filled with lemonade. He closed his eyes and went to a far-off place.

The musician's name was Rudyard Cross, a man with thick fingers, wet blue eyes, and a neatly trimmed white moustache and beard. For years Rudyard earned a living playing the Wurlitzer organ at silent film festivals all around the world. He retired to our town, the town of his own boyhood, and now performed only occasionally—at the ice rink and, at Christmastime, at Town Hall in front of the big Christmas tree. As a kid I was always being dragged by my mother and father to the lighting ceremony. Otherwise, my father wasn't the going-into-town sort of man. He didn't seem to have any friends other than my mother. He worked as a corrections officer at the East Jersey State Prison and had no patience for men who complained about their wives or their kids or long days at a cushy office. As far as I knew, my father never had a poker night with the guys, or fishing buddies. He liked watching sports on television, but always alone. It's possible that had I played Little League or football, he'd have come to cheer, but I was no athlete. He loved the tree-lighting, though, and on the ride home all he would talk about was Rudyard Cross.

"A town like ours doesn't often get a talent like that," he'd say, and my mother and I would agree. Breakneck Beach was a small town, and nobody in it seemed especially talented.

"His playing soothes me," my father would say, and I would be glad for that, but also feel that somehow I had let him down.

That was when my mother was alive. By my freshman year in high school she had been gone for three years, and my father had been promoted to senior corrections officer. Sometimes he called to let me know he'd be working late, but on Friday afternoons he always left on time so that by six o'clock he'd be showered, reclined in his chair, and waiting for Rudyard's shave-and-a-haircut knock on the front door.

The routine was simple. My father would make a request, and Rudyard would say, "What a *mar*velous suggestion," and then play it. He spoke with an accent. Even though he was from New Jersey, he sounded very formal, almost British, and a little funny. When he played, the piano sounded like a completely different instrument than when my mother had played it. The piano had been hers—inherited, I believe, from her mother—and as a girl she had taken lessons. I remember her drifting over to it and playing the simple, graceful pieces she'd learned decades earlier. Bach inventions, Mozart mazurkas, folksongs from books with fingerings penned in. I'd sit next to her on the bench and turn pages when she nodded.

Rudyard never played from music. He'd memorized

everything. And he sounded as if four or five hands were all playing at once. His style was schmaltzy, but so accomplished that schmaltzy seemed like the only style imaginable. I sat there beside him and watched his fingers moving so fast they were like blurs. His left foot, accustomed to the Wurlitzer's pedals, stamped out phantom bass lines on the carpet.

At seven o'clock, my father would thank the master musician, reach into his wallet, remove two twenties, and hand them over. "No, thank *you*, Mr. Miller," the musician would say, and tuck the bills into his shirt pocket. He'd give a funny little bow and depart. When I closed the door behind him, and it was just the two of us again, my father would size me up, frown at the result, and say, "Okay, your turn."

My turn. This had been my piano lesson, and my father wanted to hear what I had retained.

I liked to think that I had potential. It was why I had asked for the lessons to begin with. My best friend, Danny Linnard, had recently started playing the guitar, and I found myself able to pick out a couple of melodies on it. And sometimes I would try playing these same melodies on the piano. My hope was to become good enough that my father would buy me a synthesizer, and Danny and I could start a rock band.

My father didn't believe in doing things halfway. When my mother was alive, he bought her five-dozen roses on their anniversary. On Halloween, our house looked as if it had arrived straight from Hell itself. Little kids were afraid to come up our front walkway. And my father didn't drink alcohol because, in his words, you either drank or you didn't. There was a time a few years back when he did. Now, he didn't. Which was why he drank lemonade these days, and not the store-bought kind. He squeezed the lemons himself and dumped in sugar and ice water. He made vats of it.

And ever since the doctor told him to cut back on red meat, he never ate it again, which meant that I never ate it again— except for once or twice a year, when he'd come home with a couple of monstrously thick steaks that he'd grill up and we'd devour. Then we'd spend the next twenty-four hours fighting each other for the john, our stomachs in revolt.

So when I said I wanted piano lessons, my father thought for a moment and said, "You'll need a real pro," then went straight for the yellow pages. He looked up the number for the ice rink, which he called in search of Rudyard Cross. They had a brief discussion, which sent my father back to the yellow pages again, this time for a piano tuner. The piano hadn't been tuned in years, not since before my mother got sick.

Toward the end of my first lesson (major scales, the treble clef), my father came into the living room and asked Rudyard, "In your professional opinion, did this piano tuner earn his fee?" My father didn't like getting ripped off.

My new teacher took this as his cue and said, "We had better see for sure." He got up from the metal folding chair I'd brought in from the garage and sat next to me on the piano bench. He played one piece, then another. The following week, ten minutes into my second lesson, my father came into the living room, settled into his recliner, and asked Rudyard if he knew Wagner's "Ride of the Valkyries." Rudyard didn't just know it, he practically breathed it, and in the years that followed I could never hear that piece without picturing Rudyard's fifteen-minute, brow-sweating performance.

The third week, Rudyard went straight for the piano bench, and I took my place on the chair. This arrangement seemed to serve both my father and Rudyard well. My father needed calm, and Rudyard, not performing much anymore, seemed to bask in my father's admiration.

But once Rudyard was out the front door, my father

remembered what the man's alleged purpose had been in coming to our house, and I would be asked to play. With the master's music still in my ears, I would sit at the piano and try moving my hands the way it seemed that Rudyard had, flopping them around the keyboard like dying fish. Every week I did this, and every week there came a moment when I half-expected my "lessons" suddenly to click into place, and for lush and beautiful music to begin filling the house. I wanted to succeed. Seeing how Rudyard's playing could temporarily transform my father from a senior corrections officer into a placid, even blissful man, I felt inspired, and not a little envious.

I didn't retain a thing. Not musically, anyway. And yet I began to imitate my teacher's unusual affectations. His gestures, his smile, the tilt of his head, his resonant voice and sort-of-British accent. None of this was natural for me. I had always been a quiet boy. My skill of keeping underneath other people's radar had been finely honed over many years. I could stay entertained with a Stephen King novel in my bedroom, or watching TV, a bowl of pretzels on my lap. I had made it to the ninth grade without being pounded or pummeled or even shoved. And this success—not being regarded as a target, or even regarded at all—was giving me a false sense of what I could get away with.

It was around the third lesson that I began to imitate Rudyard Cross. Not in the company of my father, though. That much I learned quickly one morning at breakfast, after passing a piece of toast. My father had grumbled a thanks to me, and I stood, bowed, and said theatrically, "No, thank *you*, Mister Miller," doing my best rendition of Rudyard's strange accent.

My father stopped spreading a glob of jam on his toast and looked up at me. "Now what the hell is that?" He set his toast down. "You don't want to talk like that."

He had a way in those days of saying things that made my eyes fill with tears without warning. I remember looking down at the table, telling him that I was only kidding.

"You don't want to kid like that," he said. "You'll put your father in an early grave, kidding like that."

I wasn't entirely sure what my father meant, but I could tell that I was supposed to know. And so I saved my impression of Rudyard for school, telling the other kids how *marvelous* they were. "Benjamin, that was just *marvelous*," I said after he had solved a difficult algebra problem on the blackboard. "Mrs. Mulligan, this play is *marvelous*," I told my English teacher. We were reading Romeo and Juliet. "Isn't Shakespeare *marvelous*?" And after a few days of this, I no longer felt as if I were impersonating anybody. It felt like a new way of being myself. I had stepped out of the shadows and was using what my mother used to call a Strong Personality. She had liked Strong Personalities. The principal of the school where she worked had one. My grandfather, before he died, had one. So did my mother's favorite actor, Paul Newman. I couldn't help thinking that she would have liked the Strong Personality I was trying out these days, especially because it had sprung from music and friendliness and goodwill.

Up until then, I hadn't looked forward each morning to school. Several neighborhood schools fed into the public high school, and most of the kids were strangers to me. The juniors and seniors seemed impossibly old. They were adults, sailing down the hallways, fearless. But even the underclassmen found one another, clumping together between classes and at lunch, while Danny and I still ate together at a small table not ten feet from where the teachers sat on patrol.

Suddenly, though, other kids began talking to me, talking *like* me. They'd tell me to have a *marvelous* day. Leaving a classroom, they'd say to me, "No, I insist, after you," in that funny accent. At lunch, people I didn't even know would call my name and wave. It all seemed to be going well, until one afternoon when Danny came over to my house with his guitar to jam.

He'd been taking lessons since August at Bingo's Music, where his mother had bought him the guitar. Now, in my living room, Danny pulled the dull green electric out of its case and plugged in his small Peavey amp. It took him a while to get the guitar tuned because he'd forgotten his tuner at home. Eventually he got the strings sounding okay, and turned up the distortion. He impressed me with the opening riff to "Sweet Home Alabama." I couldn't play along, so I just pretended, keeping my hands a few inches over the piano keys while he played the riff over and over. When we got tired of that, Danny played some of the chords he'd learned. Then he stopped playing and said, "Why are you acting like such a fag?" He was still looking at the guitar strings, because he didn't want to look at me.

"What the hell do you mean?" I said.

"The way you talk," he said.

"Right now?"

"Not right now," he said. "But at school. You sound like a real fag."

I couldn't believe this was Danny talking. If anybody should have understood what a bold move it was for me to let my classmates know of my existence, it should have been him. He had made a career out of keeping under people's radar, too. "Oh yeah? Says who?"

"Everybody. That's why they're talking like you talk. Everybody's making fun of you."

I told him he didn't know what the hell he was talking about. But I thought back to my father at the breakfast table a couple of weeks ago, his strong reaction to my Strong Personality.

"All I know is," Danny said, "you should stop being so weird at school. I'm only saying so because I'm your friend."

I had been getting angry, but this direct declaration of friendship made me embarrassed. It was too genuine, too frank, and I had nothing to say in response. So I asked him to show me how to play something on the guitar.

"Fine," he said. We sat next to each other on the carpet, and he showed me how to play an E major chord. First he played it, then he handed me the guitar and placed my fingers on the frets. "Put this one here," he said. "Press here." His touch tickled a little, and I had a hard time molding my fingers into the right shapes. Finally I eked out the chord, but barely.

"You play," I said, handing him back the guitar, and he began strumming chords. As he played, I looked at him. We'd been best friends ever since the fourth grade, when our parents made us both quit Cub Scouts because the scout leader kept talking about Allah. Now, Danny had the beginnings of a moustache. Just a little. His face was looking less like a kid's face. It looked more rigid, his eyes less forgiving, and I wondered if my own face still looked the way I always thought it had.

I sat at the piano again, saddened that while Danny could actually play music, I couldn't. I was a faker. So I faked. I started banging away at the piano, and then Danny must have gotten jealous because what I was doing looked like more fun, and was a lot louder, than what he was doing. He laid down his guitar on the rug and sat beside me on the piano bench. We were both skinny and fit comfortably. I was really overdoing the Rudyard technique—swaying my body, making funny faces, flopping my wrists all over the place—and Danny said that now I *looked* like a fag. "Shut up, *Fanny*," I said, and then he started banging on the piano the same as me, our hands competing for space on the keyboard, and when I glanced over at his face for a moment, he seemed like a kid again, and I was glad. We started using our fists, hammering the keys as hard and fast as we could. The piano was reaching a cacophonous crescendo when a sharp smack on the back of my neck shook my whole spine.

My father stood tall over us, his face coated in a fine layer of sweat, stinking like a day's work, his uniform the same dark brown as his five o'clock shadow.

"What in God's name are you two doing?" he said. My neck stung and my ears rang. I could feel Danny's silence next to me.

"We're *playing*, Dad," I said. "That's what all those lessons are for, remember? *Playing?*"

He gave me, then Danny, a hard stare. Then me again. He went into the kitchen, where I heard the refrigerator open and close, and then a giant glass of lemonade being poured.

"Listen, son." My father stood in the doorway of the bathroom that night while I brushed my teeth. "When I saw you two down there, clowning around like that on the piano...just promise me you won't do it again."

I spat into the sink and wiped my mouth on a hand towel. "I didn't mean to bang so hard on the piano."

"Yeah," my father said. "And knock off that other stuff you were doing, too. Looking all silly like Mr. Cross. You don't need to do that. Acting all..." He shook his head. "I know what you were doing, and I don't like it."

I didn't like him accusing me of things. Not unless I'd actually done something wrong, like lose my sweatshirt or forget to take out the garbage. "Do you even like Mister Cross?" I asked.

"*Like* him? What kind of a question is that? He's your piano teacher. He's a professional. What does it matter whether I like him or not?"

It did matter to him, though. Because come Friday night, while I was on the folding chair and Rudyard Cross was at the piano, lost in the music and doing an impression of me doing an impression of him, my father was practically having a seizure. No matter how hard he tried, he couldn't sit still. He kept shifting in his seat, and clearing his throat, and at one point his drink went down the wrong pipe and he started coughing like mad. A few minutes later he spilled his drink and I had to run into the kitchen for paper towels. He sighed loudly while I wiped up the rug. Rudyard kept glancing over at us, but he was a professional and kept playing.

After barely a half-hour, my father thanked Rudyard and said, "I think we'll call it a night." He followed Rudyard out onto the front step and closed the door behind them. I eavesdropped from inside and heard every word.

"Look," my father said, "I don't want you teaching my kid anymore." His voice had an edge to it that I heard only rarely. He sounded older, and very official—probably his work voice. "You've come into our house and done your job, but now it's time to call it quits. Understood?"

"Mister Miller, is there a problem? Because whatever it is—"

"There's no problem. But Brandon won't be needing any more lessons." I knew right away this had to do with the way I'd behaved with Danny at the piano, and yet nothing to do with music. I wondered if he had heard about the way I was behaving at school. I wished I could explain to him that I had already put my Strong Personality to rest. Danny was right, I had decided. Other kids were making fun of me. It was time to become reacquainted with my talent for lying low. "I think Brandon has learned quite enough from you," my father said.

"Oh, Mister Miller, it's just as well," Rudyard said angrily. "The boy has very little talent." I yanked back the curtain covering the small window beside the door and saw Rudyard shaking his head. "I didn't mean that. It's the holiday stress. I'm sure you can understand."

My father nodded. "Let's just shake hands and part like gentlemen."

They shook hands, and Rudyard walked to his car, and my father came inside again. I pretended to enter the front hallway from the other room. "He's stressed?" my father said, knowing full well I'd overheard them. "*He's* stressed? The man plays the organ at an ice rink. He should try keeping killers from bashing each other's heads in. He should try stopping a man from slicing off his own genitals."

After an awkward dinner during which my father and I ate vegetarian Chinese takeout without looking at each other, I called Danny from my room and asked him if he could go to a movie tonight. And if his mom could drive us.

I'd barely said two words to him all week. He'd started eating at a new lunch table.

"Can't," he said. "Too much homework."

"How about tomorrow? I'll see whatever you want."

"Can't," he said. "Look, I'm in the middle of dinner, okay?"

"Okay." Hanging up, I wondered if I'd ever hear from him again.

A minute later, he called back. "Look, I'm going to Megan Lemming's party tomorrow night. You can come if you want."

Megan Lemming was a sophomore, and her parties were a very big deal. Everything I knew about them came from overhearing conversations on Monday mornings. Megan's father and step-mother lived at the edge of town, on several acres that used to be a farm. They didn't seem to care that each weekend their house and yard were taken over by throngs of teenagers. Maybe they were simply cool. Or maybe they'd been unpopular as kids and were trying to make up for it now.

Somehow Danny had been invited. That, or he was

crashing. Either way, I was impressed. "Sure," I told him. "Definitely. Count me in."

I knew I'd have to lie to my father about the party, afraid that he wouldn't let me go if he thought there'd be drinking. But I also didn't want him getting his hopes up, thinking I'd suddenly turned into a kid who got invited to parties. And for all I knew we'd be there for ten minutes, feel uncomfortable, and Danny would have to call his mom to pick us up. Since I wasn't a very good liar, I waited until the next afternoon, when my father was absorbed in a hockey game on TV. I said I was going with Danny to the movies later tonight. He grunted, and that was that.

Danny had arranged a ride with a couple of juniors he knew from shop class. He had told me nine o'clock, but nine o'clock came and went, as did nine-thirty and ten and ten-thirty. By then I had stopped looking out the living-room window. I sat on my bed and took a hard look at my bedroom—the sports car lamp, the Star Wars action figures—and remembered that Danny had a poster on his wall of a woman in a bikini. On my wall was a poster of a penguin wearing sunglasses, telling me to "Be Cool." No question, I had the bedroom of a child. A baby, practically. I wanted to tear that poster off the wall, ball it up and throw it in the trash, but my mother had given it to me. And I sort of liked it. So I just sat there and brooded, listening to the TV drone on downstairs, and every so often checking the digital clock on my night table.

I was rehearsing an invective against Danny for Monday morning, a snide account of his so-called friendship, when I heard the chummy *beep-beep* of a car horn. I shot out of my room and downstairs, yelled to my father that I'd see him later, and before he could growl something about it being too late for me to leave, I ran outside, where it was crisp and dry and felt vaguely electric.

"What's up, man," Danny said as I crawled in the back

seat beside him. He didn't ever call me *man*, and I appreciated that he was trying to sound cool and draw me into his coolness. "What's up," I said, having forgiven him completely, as the car pulled away from the curb.

"Guys, this is Brandon Miller," Danny said. "This is Darius and Nick." I recognized them from Danny's new lunch table. "Hey," I said.

"How's it hanging, Miller?" asked Darius, who was driving.

"Cool, man," I said, making my voice deep and indifferent. "What's up with you?" But Darius was so cool he didn't answer.

Danny had on a denim jacket I'd never seen before—I felt certain it was new—but I wasn't going to embarrass him and mention it. I hadn't worn a coat, because my fall jacket made me look like I had walked off the set of Mister Rogers. I would rather freeze. I wore jeans and a baggy gray shirt that made it hard to tell how skinny I was. I'd put conditioner in my hair and sprayed a ton of Right Guard under my arms. I was as ready for a party as I would ever be.

Danny reached down on the floor and came up with a can of Meister Bräu. He cracked it open and took a swig, belched theatrically, then handed the can to me. It was as if Danny had an alternate life I knew nothing about. If this was an act, I was fooled. I accepted the beer from him and took my first-ever sip. When it didn't taste as bad as I'd always expected, I drank a little more.

"Whoa there, Brandon," Danny said, and took back the can.

Nick, who sat in the front passenger seat, worked the radio dial. Both he and Darius wore school jackets. I didn't know what sport they played, but I was too nervous to ask, so I kept my mouth shut. Anyway, the music was too loud for talk.

Eventually we reached the Lemmings' long driveway. A rustic wooden fence bordered the property, and various shrubs and trees obscured the house, set back several hundred feet from the road. As soon as Darius had parked the car, he and Nick were off, jogging across the grass in the dark toward the house, leaving me and Danny to walk together up the path. A number of kids were near a side door, including Megan Lemming. She wore jeans with patches all over them, and a leather jacket. A cigarette dangled from her lips. She sized us up. "Nice jacket, Danny," she said, and the girl beside her giggled. "It's three dollars for the keg." We paid her. "You may enter," she said. When we did, I could feel the wisecracks trailing in our wake.

We followed the thumping of music into the basement, which was crammed with kids. The basement was unfinished except that the cinder-block walls were painted bright yellow, and on the floor were mismatched sections of carpets. Black-lights made everybody's teeth and clothes glow. These were the same people who flooded the hallways at school, but all the sensations were strange. The smoke and incense made breathing hard, and the music pounded out an angry dance beat, and the lighting cast shadows that made even the people I recognized seem unfamiliar.

A number of sofas and end tables bordered the room. On the sofa nearest the stairway, a girl straddled a boy and they were making out. Before I made myself look away, I couldn't help staring at them, at their hair enmeshed, at the boy's hands moving lower and lower down the girl's back. A ping-pong table in the middle of the room was covered with plastic cups of beer, some full, many empty. In one corner a crowd gathered around what I assumed was the keg.

This was where Danny led me, past a sofa on which sat three girls including Amanda Van Sickle, who had been popular in junior high, whose talent had been yelling at teachers without getting in trouble. For three years I don't think she ever said a word to me besides *dork*. Yet here, now, she threw her arms around me—so quickly and forcefully that I lost my balance—and before I knew it I was on her lap. "Look at me!" she announced. "I've got Brandon Miller and I'm not letting go!" She squeezed me tight as I teetered on her lap. "You know, Miller, you've got a bony butt." She put a hand behind my head and pushed her face into mine, kissing me hard on the lips. Kissing a girl felt a lot different than I had thought it would. It was wetter and tasted more like liquor. I tried to pull away because she was embarrassing me, but she wasn't lying—she wasn't letting me go. The girls beside us shrieked. When Amanda finally released me, I sprang up like a jack-in-the-box and felt my face burning. The party was so large, though, everybody moving in many directions at once, that people didn't seem to have noticed us. Nobody cared.

But I cared. I felt like the party's mascot, the dog you throw a silly hat on for Halloween. I wanted to say something to let Amanda know that I was her equal, that I was in high school, too, but she was already yelling something to her friends about a guy named Steve, and I was forgotten. Danny was over by the keg, so I went there myself and waited forever for a cupful of beer. I watched how kids pumped the tap so the beer came out, and when it was my turn I did the same. I drank pretty fast and then without saying one word to anybody I waited some more to refill my cup. Danny stood right there beside me, but you would never know we were friends. We were like travelers standing on a train platform, looking left and right to see where the train might be.

Eventually my stomach started to feel full. I had refilled my cup two more times and started to lose my fear of anybody making fun of me. I pumped the handle on the tap while people refilled their cups. I pretended to be a bartender at an exclusive party, like on a cruise ship. "Enjoy your beverage," I started saying to people, forgetting that

I'd given up my Strong Personality. "Enjoy this *mar*velous brew." I was smiling at my classmates, refilling their cups, every now and then refilling my own, ignoring my full stomach. I pumped the hell out of that tap for the longest time, until the rubber hose started spewing desperate bursts of foam, and then nothing at all.

People watched in horror, until a guy came forward and took the nozzle from my hand. He bent over the keg and lifted it up in the air a foot or two, and slammed it down again into the tub of ice.

"Keg's kicked."

Word spread, and within minutes the music was off, the lights on, and people began to leave. I didn't see Danny. But when Darius, Nick and I went outside, there he was, seated on the back steps talking to Rachel Flint, the sophomore who gave morning announcements. She had short black hair and a perfect little nose. "We're driving Rachel home," Danny said, and in the car the two of them scrunched together even though the backseat wasn't *that* crowded.

Soon we were all complaining about the keg getting kicked so early.

"It's barely one a.m.," Nick said. "I'm still sober, for God sakes. I'm fucking sober."

"No, you aren't," Darius said.

"Still." Nick turned around in his seat, leaned over us, and shouted, "Is this the party car?" When we didn't answer right away, he repeated louder, "Is this the *party* car, yes or no?"

Danny and Rachel weren't even listening. They were having some other conversation. So I shouted, "Yes!"

"No," Nick said, "it isn't. Not without beer."

We pulled into a strip mall and stopped in the fire lane outside the A&P Liquors. Darius asked which of us had fake ID. A ludicrous question. Nobody in the back seat looked even remotely close to twenty-one.

Danny's right thumb—which had been lying flat on the seat along with the rest of his hand—began to rub Rachel's leg, and she seemed to be letting him.

"Wait here," I said. When I got out of the car, the world spun around me and I almost fell to my knees. I kept my sights on the glass door and walked toward it. I hadn't ever been in a liquor store before, but it was easy enough to find a twelve-pack of cans. On the check-out line stood a half-dozen silent, tired-looking people. Behind the counter, a small man with white hair and sunken cheeks punched numbers slowly on the register without looking up. I took a step toward the door and hesitated. Then I pictured Danny's thumb wagging back and forth against Rachel's jeans, and went for it. No waiting in line—just straight out the door. I imagined sirens. Policemen from out of nowhere shoving me to the ground, hauling me off to the place where my father worked. *Something.* Instead, there was utter calm as I returned to the car, tossed the beer into the backseat, and got in myself. "Here."

"Damn—how'd you get that?" Danny asked.

"I got it successfully," I said.

With nowhere to go, we went back to Megan Lemming's street and parked in the driveway. The yard was dark and still, and we all stood around and opened beers. My teeth were chattering but I didn't feel freezing. I felt amazed. At some point later tonight I would tell everybody exactly how I had acquired the beer. For now, the five of us stood in a clump, just drinking. We weren't all friends, and nobody really knew what to say. At one point I asked Darius and Nick what sport they played, and they asked what I meant, and I said the jackets, and then they looked down at the ground, and Nick said trombone, and Darius said French horn.

Away from the forced closeness of the backseat, Danny was losing ground with Rachel. A couple of times he asked her questions, but her answers were terse and dismissive.

The word "curfew" got mentioned. (To me the word sounded strange and remarkably cinematic. I had no curfew. There had never been a need.) At one point, Darius told Rachel that he knew how to waltz, and they started waltzing. Danny looked really unhappy about it, so I said, "Guess how I got the beer? Hey, stop waltzing for a second and listen to how I got the beer." And I told them.

For ten seconds I was king, everybody laughing and saying *No way* and *bullshit* and *get out of here.* It got quiet again, and that was when Danny said it.

The night was ending—we were probably about ready to leave—but he *said* it: "That was *mar*velous of you, Brandon. Simply *mar*velous." Not only did he say it, he flicked both his wrists, like I did when I pretended to play the piano, only worse, and everyone laughed.

"Fuck you, Danny," I said, and walked away from the car, into the Lemmings' dark field.

Danny followed me. "What?" he said. "I was only kidding. Jesus, Brandon, I was kidding."

We stopped walking. I know I was crying a little, because the cold air was making my eyes freeze. My stomach hurt, and the earth's spinning was getting more intense. I asked Danny if he was my friend.

"What? Sure, man," he said. "Of course I am."

"Yeah?"

"Yeah."

Looking at Danny, my thoughts flashed to Amanda grabbing me at the party solely because it was what she felt like doing, not caring if it was what I had wanted, or how I might take it. There's been no planning. She'd simply *acted.* I thrust a hand behind Danny's head, and in the darkness of Megan Lemming's front yard, I kissed him. Hard, but quick.

After, he breathed heavily three times—I'll never forget those three burdened sighs—and then he punched me in the gut.

I'd have punched him back, but he knocked the wind out of me, and I was down for a minute with my arms around my stomach, gasping. By the time I could breathe again I was crying pretty steadily. Everybody was calling to me in the dark to come back to the car, but I wouldn't. Even when Rachel asked nicely, I told her no way, and to leave me the hell alone.

Once they'd all given up on me and driven away, I decided to walk up to the Lemmings' house and ring their doorbell and call my father. He'd kill me for being out so late, and kill me again for being drunk. But when you're fourteen and in need of a ride and a bed, your options are limited.

Halfway up the driveway I threw up for the longest time, then kept walking to the front porch. I had to keep ringing their doorbell, but eventually Mr. Lemming opened the door in a bathrobe, looking very tired. He led me into the kitchen, told me to sit down, and asked for my phone number. He called my dad for me and suggested that I stay here overnight. "No, nothing's out of control," Mr. Lemming said into the phone. "It's late and he needs some sleep, is all." I hoped Mr. Lemming would continue to be vague, but then he said, "Believe me, it won't be the first time one of Megan's friends sobered up in the guest room." I cringed. Then he made it even worse: "But that's being a teenager, isn't it? Drinking, smoking." *Smoking?* That my father agreed to let me stay only confirmed the depths of his displeasure. Were he to come get me now, his voice would wake everyone in the house as he lit into not only me, but Mr. Lemming for running such a loose ship.

Mr. Lemming showed me to the guest room, set a trashcan by the bed, and told me that my father said he'd be here at eight a.m. sharp. "He's an intense man, your father," Mr. Lemming said, and left me alone.

The clock on the night table said 3:30. Despite the trashcan, I spent most of the next few hours in the bathroom, over the toilet. Their house was large, but everyone probably heard me. Kneeling on the tile floor, my throat on fire, I tried not to think about facing my father, or kissing Danny, or the icy look on his face just before he punched me, or how an evening can turn on you so quickly.

I wondered if my mother would have insisted on coming for me, taking me home. If she'd have gone back to bed or stayed up with me while I barfed, telling me it was my own fault but without a tinge of deep disappointment. If she'd have asked, *What happened tonight?* And if I'd have told her. But I had no idea what my mother would have said or done. I never would. At her funeral the pastor told me that when I remembered my mother, she wouldn't look like she had in the end. She would always look healthy and beautiful in my mind. But that wasn't really true. Sometimes when I remembered her she looked healthy, but sometimes not. Sometimes she looked bony and ashen, her eyes too big in their sockets. But right now I couldn't see her at all. Her face, which I tried hard to pin down, kept swirling right along with the room, the house, the world.

At seven o'clock I smeared toothpaste on my tongue and rinsed, went downstairs and outside, and started walking down the driveway to wait. I saw where I'd thrown up hours earlier. The wind had picked up, and soon my teeth were chattering.

When my father pulled in the driveway an hour later, he lowered the passenger window and asked if I had remembered to apologize to Mr. and Mrs. Lemming. "Yes," I said, even though I hadn't. But I *was* sorry. More than that, I was cold, and very tired.

My father looked tired himself, with heavy eyes and messy hair, wearing his Jets sweatshirt that was older than I was.

"Good," he said. "Now get in the goddamn car."

As we backed out of the driveway, I raised the passenger window and cranked up the heat. I was shivering big time.

Despite the toothpaste my mouth tasted nasty, and my throat still burned, and all I wanted was a long shower and my own bed.

My father had the car radio playing softly. Even with Thanksgiving still over a week away, a Christmas song was on—one I didn't know, with sappy lines about sleigh bells and holly. Plenty of schmaltz. I pictured our lively living room and how, come next Friday, it would be vacant and without song. And I wondered if my father pictured this, too, and regretted firing Rudyard Cross. Or knowing him, if he'd already moved on to the logistics of getting the piano out of the house entirely.

We listened to "White Christmas" and "Sleigh Ride" and "Jingle Bell Rock." God knows why this station was so intent on rushing the year. It wasn't so bad, though. The music and the heat made me feel much younger, like we were home again with my mother and a tree with dopey ornaments, where everybody felt safe. I closed my eyes and went there for a while.

THE CASTLE OF HORRORS

Jane Tanner, dead almost three weeks, tried to murder him again, this time with a pirate's sword. Russell, who worked security at the Castle of Horrors, was seated in his corner of the Texas Chainsaw Massacre room when Jane rushed him. There was no need to dodge out of the way. Jane's control with the sword was, as usual, awful. Her wild swing missed him by several feet.

"Next time I'll eviscerate you!" she hissed.

He sighed, and reminded her that the weapons were only styrofoam props that the actors used to scare the patrons. She frowned as if this were news and tried ramming the sword into her own chest. It went straight through her body and dropped harmlessly to the floor.

"Dammit," she said, "you're right. That didn't hurt at all." She sat down on the carpet to sulk. "I'm still going to kill you, though," she said.

"I know you are, Jane."

"Make your kids orphans, like you made mine."

She always remembered that part. Other particulars confused her: she'd forget that the Castle of Horrors wasn't the entire universe. She thought Russell's name was Bronco.

But the fact that her two young children were all alone,

and that Russell had caused it to happen? No confusion there.

"I don't have any kids," Russell said.

"Ah, but you would, if I let you live."

"I don't think so. I never really planned on having them."

"Not yet," she said. "Soon, though, you and Claire would have gone on to have four children." Claire was the name of the woman whom Russell would supposedly fall in love with. "Three sons and a daughter." Her eyes narrowed. "Don't look at me all skeptical." She smacked Russell on the leg. This was progress for her—a week earlier, her hand would have passed right through him. "I know these things."

"Whatever you say."

"Don't whatever *me*, Bronco. Don't condescend. I'm from the goddamn beyond."

He was a man born to work security. Six-six, two hundred and eighty pounds, with thick hands and the kind of severe gaze that made people aware of their full bladders. But eventually you get tired of tossing drunk assholes out of the Pink Pony strip club. You long for a little happiness. Besides, when you get a DUI and they take away your driver's license, you need to find a job you can bike to, and you need to do it fast. Especially when you already owe back-rent.

His piece-of-shit car barely sold and got him only enough cash for the month's utilities and a halfway decent mountain bike. Things looked bleak. But when one of the regulars at the Pink Pony started bellyaching about losing his security gig at Smitty's Arcade, Russell's ears perked up. The arcade was part of Happy Land, built on the old Breakneck Beach fishing pier. Despite living just a mile inland, Russell hadn't been to the pier for years. But he had fond memoires of climbing down to the sand underneath the pier to smoke weed and watch the waves.

"So why'd you get canned?" Russell asked.

"Now that's a fair question, Russ." The man set his beer on the bar. "So you know how, like, I'm *here* a lot?" He belched. "Well, there you go."

The next afternoon, Russell rode his bike to the pier. The life-giving sun warmed his face as he walked the midway. These last six years, since eking out the high-school diploma, he'd worked in a number of dark bars, and he'd almost forgotten what it was like to hear the surf and smell the Italian sausages frying and feel the salty breeze on his face. Today was Saturday, and the amusement pier buzzed with families who actually seemed to be enjoying themselves.

He walked into Smitty's Arcade in high spirits, remembering how as a kid he'd blown countless quarters here playing Skee-ball, pinball, this-ball and that-ball, games where you'd race a car or shoot aliens, and, if you were skilled enough, get to type in your initials—or if she was watching you, the initials of the girl you had a crush on.

Yes, he could definitely work here.

Except, he couldn't.

"Who the hell said I was hiring?" asked the manager, once Russell had tracked him down behind the prize counter.

"Guy named Goober?" Russell said.

"That putz? Yeah, I fired him like three months ago." He took a small stack of tickets from a boy, counted them, and exchanged them for a spider ring. "Look, I heard the Castle might be looking for somebody. You should check with Angie."

Ten minutes later he was in the employee-only area behind the Castle of Horrors, hearing from Angie Bailey that, yes, she was hiring.

"You're really big," she said. "I mean, Jesus." Angie herself was barely five feet tall and looked like a wet bird.

"Yup," he said. "That's my talent."

Angie led him through the walk-through haunted house,

his enthusiasm for landing this new job undercut by the fact that once again he'd be working in a dim, dreary place. Take the Texas Chainsaw Massacre room: the room was pitch dark except for the black-light illuminating five mannequins seated at a dinner table. One of the mannequins had on a scraggly blond wig. Her wrists were bound to the chair, and her painted-on eyes were enormous; her terror looked absolutely genuine. There must have been speakers hidden somewhere, but the screams seemed to come from the mannequin. The others at the table—her captors—screamed in mocking response. And then, just like in the movie, they began to laugh while she went on screaming.

"What are they made out of, wax?" Russell asked.

"Plastic," she said. "Pretty realistic, though, don't you think?"

"A little too realistic."

Angie smiled. "This is where you'll be stationed." She nodded toward the dinner table. "Say hello to your co-workers."

As Angie led him through the Graveyard, the Nightmare Tavern, the Rabid Swamp and the rest of the Castle's many rooms, Russell met his real-life co-workers, the dozen or so employees who dressed up like monsters and vampires and famous killers and roamed around terrorizing the patrons.

Once they were through the Rat Tunnel and back behind the Castle again, Angie gave Russell a time sheet and some tax forms. "I'll see you tomorrow," she said, and went back inside.

There was a girl leaning against the pier's railing, smoking a cigarette. She had on a wig of long, black hair with a silver streak running through it. Ghoulish theatrical makeup made her face sinister and shadowy, and fake blood covered her skimpy costume.

"I take it you're the new security," she said.

"That's right," he said. "So who're you supposed to be?"

"Lizzie Borden." She smiled, but it was impossible to see her real expression behind all the makeup. In this way, she could have been any of the girls at the Pink Pony.

"You like working in there?" he asked.

"Are you kidding? I love it." So there was the difference. She flicked ashes off the pier. "Trust me, before long it'll feel like home."

To celebrate, he ordered a slice of pizza and a twenty-ounce beer. He hung around the midway and even slapped down two dollars to toss Wiffle balls at colored cups and maybe win a giant stuffed zebra. He didn't win the zebra, but he won a Chinese finger trap.

"Look, it's nothing personal," Russell explained to his boss that night at the Pink Pony. "It's just this DUI. Plus, I fucking hate it here." He hadn't realized how true it was until he'd said it.

"Hey, come on now," his boss said. "You owe me better than that."

When he'd first started working at the Pink Pony, Russell had just turned twenty-two and still had no clue how to hold on to a job. His worst habit was falling in love with the dancers every two seconds. Then one of his big-time crushes, a part-time nursing student with a baby at home, got beaten up in the parking lot one night. In the days that followed, Russell became overzealous in his bouncer duties. His boss had been patient, though, drilling it into Russell's head that he couldn't exact revenge on every smug musclehead who strutted into the club.

"You got to detach yourself," his boss had said at the time. "Detachment—that's a life strategy I just gave you, son."

It had been wise counsel, and maybe Russell did owe his boss better. But the boardwalk was pulling him. "Everyone's always smiling all the time around here," Russell said now.

It was true: a strip club was the smiliest place on earth. "But I haven't seen a single happy person in years. Do you see what I'm saying?"

Earlier, he'd given his Chinese finger trap to a kid who kept chucking his Wiffle balls at the wrong cups. The kid's smile had been the real deal.

"When the summer ends, you can't come back," his boss said. "I'll have a replacement by then. You understand?"

Russell shrugged. "There's always a bar looking for a guy my size, am I right?"

His boss looked at him a moment, face frozen, then flashed his teeth like a game-show host. "You just burned a bridge, my friend." He was a thin-necked man in his fifties who went around shooting his customers with an imaginary pistol, like they were in on some joke but deserved to die because of it. "Burned it right up."

The Texas Chainsaw room was located on the second floor of the Castle. Russell's job entailed sitting in the corner, in his black jeans and black t-shirt, and watching the customers enter one end of the room and leave the other.

Talk about an easy gig. The setting did all the work. Even the bravest customers felt queasy walking through the cemetery, the Rat Tunnel, ducking under Lizzie Borden's swinging axe. Their eyes were worthless, especially during daytime when their pupils were tiny pinpricks from the sun. So they'd creep through the Castle, snapping their heads from side to side, bracing themselves.

Still, Russell was needed. Every so often there'd be a kid out to vandalize the displays, or some asshole out to impress his girlfriend by harassing the actors. When this happened, Russell would get word on the walkie-talkie he wore on his belt. He would melt out of the walls, just one more of the Castle's illusions, to find the troublemaker and escort him to the nearest fire exit.

No question, a good summer job. Only the actors had it better, getting paid to roam the Castle and freak people out. Now *that* looked like fun. But Angie ran a tight ship with inviolable rules: she taught her actors how to scare people during the day versus at night, how to scare a group of children versus a group of children with a parent versus a group of teenage boys versus teenage girls versus teenage coed versus a guy/girl couple versus a group of older guys. She'd been the manager here a long time and had it down to a science, how to give everybody a thrill without sending anyone to the hospital or their lawyer, and she'd made it clear to Russell on his first day that he was *not* one of the actors. He should never try to frighten the patrons, just like the actors were taught never to play security guard.

He obeyed the warning for nearly a month. Then one of the actors radioed him about that damn group of drunk teenagers. One of them had just shoved Lizzy Borden into a wall.

They're in Frankenstein's Lab right now, squawked the radio. *We need you to get them out of here, Russ.*

Will do, he radioed back.

Rowdy teenagers were a dime a dozen, but most of them knew better than to assault the employees. No, these were a particular breed of assholes, the ones who in a couple of years would come to the Pink Pony and stick their hands where they don't belong and follow the dancers out to their cars at four a.m. with their box-cutters and steel-toed boots.

Frankenstein's Lab was just a couple of rooms away from the Texas Chainsaw room. Rather than go after them, Russell decided to stay in his corner, where he would be invisible, and wait. He would eject them from the park, but first he would give them a taste of what real fright was about.

Half a minute later, they entered the room.

From deep inside himself, Russell released a thunderous bellow and leapt.

When he landed, he found himself facing not a group of teenagers, but rather two small children and a young woman about Russell's age who, seeing Russell, dropped her purse, opened her mouth as if to scream, and then, as if thinking better of it, curled into a crouch on the floor. Before Russell could ask why she was crouching on the floor, she rolled over onto her back.

The two children stood in place, clutching each other. The little girl's hair was in pigtails. The boy had on a NY Giants t-shirt that came down to his knees. They looked like nice kids, the sort you wished were yours, except their mouths looked too big for their faces because they were howling. Their howls blended with the room's screams, which then became hideous laughter. Russell crouched over the woman, still wondering where the hell those rowdy teenagers were. He looked into the eyes that were looking into his, and he thought he saw the woman grimace a little, like she'd just remembered something unpleasant. Then she stopped grimacing, yet her eyes were still wide open, and Russell had the creeping feeling that the woman who was staring at him had just died of fright.

She had.

No one that day learned exactly what had happened in the Castle of Horrors. Everyone figured: scary place, heart attack, end of story. Also, Russell might have implied that he'd watched the lady collapse from his chair in the corner of the room.

The police, the actors, they all treated Russell kindly, what with him being the first on the scene, the one to radio over to Angie that she needed to call 911. He knew a little CPR, and he explained—truthfully—how he had tried the mouth-to-mouth thing, the chest-pumping thing, until a cop who'd been patrolling Happy Land's midway came and took over.

He left out the part about the woman's breath smelling like pepperoni pizza, and how he kept worrying about crushing the dying woman's ribs with his fat, useless hands.

You did your best, Russell, everyone was telling him once the EMTs had carted the young lady away. Trailing behind them was Lizzie Borden—in real life Stacey something, a local college student—with an arm around each of the dead lady's kids. Despite her heavy theatrical makeup and fake blood, they clung to her like she was their closest kin.

You tried, man.

They all said this, except for Angie. She didn't accuse him outright, but as he was leaving to go home—the Castle closed early for the day—she called him aside. They were in the employee-only area behind the Castle. They walked over to the edge of the pier. The tide was out, and crisp waves were breaking on the beach, perfect for body-surfing. Russell realized that despite living so close to the ocean, he hadn't been swimming for years.

"I'll only ask you this once," she said. "Is there anything you feel like getting off your chest?"

He waited a moment, watching the waves, the sea gulls trailing after a party boat that must have had a good day fishing. "Not that I can think of."

She nodded. "Then go home. Get some sleep. I'll see you tomorrow."

He went home but didn't go to sleep before drinking all the booze in the apartment, right down to the sample-size mouthwash he'd gotten the last time he'd been to the dentist. He paced his basement apartment, shouting at the walls and reliving the afternoon—he couldn't get out of his mind how frightened the woman had been, and then how dead— and he considered calling morgues, finding out the woman's name, calling her husband and apologizing. But he knew he wouldn't do that any sooner than he'd return to the Castle of Horrors. That place was finished for him now. Another bridge badly burned.

Bed was a comfortable place, he decided, where you couldn't kill anyone. He would have liked to stay there forever, but he only lasted a week.

What finally roused him were the three harsh raps on his front door. The meaning, unambiguous. Sure enough, the eviction notice had been slid under his door. His landlady, who lived in the apartment upstairs, must have taken his failure to leave the house as a show of bad faith. At the bottom of the typed letter, she had scribbled: GET OUT, YOU LAZY BIG OAF!

He showered, put on his black clothes, and rode his bike over to Happy Land, where he sought out Angie in her office and pled his case: *All fucked up from watching the lady die...sort of went on a bender...slept for a week...evicted...no home, no money, no one to turn to...* It wasn't so much a case, he realized, as it was a summary of his sad existence.

Angie listened, expressionless. Her office doubled as the Castle's sound room. From it, she controlled the music and sound effects for each of the Castle's exhibits. In the sound room itself, where the guests never went, Frank Sinatra was crooning about how the best was yet to come.

"I need to know if you plan on pulling any more disappearing acts," she said.

"Not a chance," Russell said. "Actually, I was wondering..." He had practiced on the ride over, but now his request sounded foolish. She'd never go for it. "I know we've got this bathroom back here, with the changing room and shower and all." He waited, to see if she'd get the hint. He pressed on. "So I was wondering, if I were to buy an air mattress...if, you know, temporarily, I could..." He coughed. "It would be like having free security all night long."

The song ended, and then Sinatra asked to be flown to

the moon. An entire verse passed before she said, "Temporarily."

"Really?" Russell said. "Damn, thanks a lot." Angie was pushing thirty, with a hard face and small, suspicious eyes. In a slasher flick, she'd be the stern, not-so-good-looking girl who was still alive when the final credits rolled. But the rumor was that she had started screwing the sixteen-year-old custodian, so maybe that had softened her up a little. Russell struggled to put his gratitude into words. He wasn't used to forming sentences having to do with generosity and kindness.

Before he could figure out what to say, Angie stopped the CD mid-song, fixed her gaze on him, and said that she would be reducing his pay. "And I suggest you get your ass back to work, as in pronto, before I change my mind."

The dead woman's full name was Jane Elizabeth Tanner. The obituary, taped to the wall by the time clock, said it all: devoted mother, revered seventh-grade science teacher, volunteer at the ASPCA.

She would be missed by family, students, and puppies.

Russell was thinking, as he walked through the Castle toward his station, that he would need to forget all about this Jane Elizabeth Tanner. It was terrible, what had happened, but now he needed to put it out of his mind— especially if this was going to be his temporary home.

As he entered the Texas Chainsaw room, a woman sprang out of a shadowy corner and ran at him with an outthrust hatchet. As he sidestepped, the hatchet slid out of the woman's hands. He was about to restrain her when he recognized who it was and stopped in his tracks.

She had on the same Seton Hall sweatshirt as the last time he'd seen her. Same pair of tapered jeans and white canvas sneakers. She stood just a few feet from him, breathing heavily, looking like an overstressed mom in a supermarket parking lot who'd forgotten where she'd left her car.

"Oh, hell no." Russell squeezed his eyes shut and opened them again. She was still there. "I did *not* sign up for this." He watched her—part horrified, part fascinated—as she walked over to the hatchet, picked it up, and came running at him again. "Hey, cut that out!" he said, even though the weapon was only a prop.

"Don't tell me what to do!" But she didn't get far with the hatchet this time either; it slipped through her hands, which were translucent. So she went to slap him on the arm. This he allowed, but her hand went right through him and he didn't feel a thing.

She looked down at the floor and started sniffling.

To make her feel better, he rubbed his arm as if she'd bruised it a little.

"I see what you're doing," the deceased said. "Don't make fun of me."

He stopped rubbing. "Listen, I just read the obituary. I really feel like shit. I mean, I *really* feel—"

"*You* feel? Who the hell cares how you feel?" She went over and sat down on Russell's chair, leaving him to stand awkwardly beside her. "My God, I teach all year, then I spend the summer doing oil changes, rotating tires, working with sexist jerks and never seeing my kids...but I'm making ends meet, you know? I'm making it work. So I decide to call in sick and take them to Happy Land—which is no Six Flags, as you and I both know."

Sometimes the strippers at the Pink Pony would spill their guts like this to Russell. They called him a good listener, but he didn't see how standing around awkwardly and not saying much constituted good listening.

"But my kids," she went on, "they're good kids, you know? So they thank me like we're on some great vacation. And do you know what, Bronco? It *was* great. Best day since I can remember, because I was spending it with my kids. And then *you* had to—" She looked over at the dinner table, where the screaming audio loop had just started again, and then back at Russell. "How could you do this to me? I mean, what kind of sick—"

"It was an accident," he said. "I thought you were a group of delinquents."

"Do I *look* like a group of delinquents?"

Just then, three girls, all around twelve or thirteen, ran into the room holding hands with one another. Seeing them, Jane cowered into a tight ball.

The girls raced through the room and out the other side, barely glancing at the dinner table scene and totally oblivious to Russell and Jane. They were trying to get through the Castle as fast as possible. This was common, kids not wanting to *be* here, but wanting to *have been* here, so afterward they could buy the t-shirt that says "I survived the Castle of Horrors at Happy Land" and show it off to their friends.

"Anyway," Russell said once the girls were gone, "you must have had some congenital heart thing." Jane had uncoiled herself and was panting from the close call. "No one's supposed to get a heart attack at your age."

She waved his words away. "What are you, a doctor? My kids are orphans now."

"What about their—"

"Dead. Five years. Hit and run." The obituary hadn't mentioned a surviving husband; Russell had figured she was divorced. "God, I hate people." She got out of the chair and went to pick up the hatchet, which was still lying on the floor beside them, but her hands kept passing through it.

His whole shift, Jane didn't leave him alone for a minute. When she wasn't trying to kick him in the shins, she was taunting him with the sweet, sweet life he would not be allowed to live. Only when someone else came into the room— patrons, or one of the actors—did she let up. She was afraid of scaring anyone, of doing to them what Russell had done to her, and so she would dart underneath the dinner table and hide there trembling until the coast was clear.

Otherwise, she prattled on breathlessly: Russell would have fallen in love and gotten his heart crushed big-time by an amateur bowler, but then he would have met Claire. They would have married in Vegas, but their drive-through wedding would not have been Elvis-themed. They would have seen Venice but not Rome. Their son would one day have thrown a baseball through the kitchen window, and instead of becoming angry Russell would have taken photographs.

His wife would have aged gracefully.

He would have known happiness.

None of this sounded like him at all. "I think you might have me confused with someone else," he told her.

"I don't think so," Jane replied. "But it doesn't really matter. You'll be dead soon anyway."

Then she'd detail the methods she was considering. Russell figured she must have been a good science teacher, because she knew exactly which chemicals would do the most damage to his private anatomy.

At ten p.m. the park closed for the night. The appeal of sleeping overnight in the Castle had diminished significantly. Russell wished he hadn't sold his car. And the boardwalk benches were too short for him. There was always the beach, he supposed.

Angie stood at the picnic table behind the Castle, by the pier's edge. She was painting a second coat on some new styrofoam knives. The northern half of the sky was rust-colored from the New York City night. To the east, lights from a smattering of boats looked like stars that had dipped below the horizon.

Russell was about to sneak out for the night when she caught his eye. "Listen—while you were away, there's been some minor damage to a couple of the displays. It's happening overnight. I'm thinking rodents might have found a way in. Anyway, keep an eye out, will you?"

He nodded, imagining Jane alone in the Castle at night, finding her way around. "Will do."

"You're a good man, Russ."

He was glad that she looked back down at the knife she was painting, because his strained smile must have been straight out of the Pink Pony.

When she wasn't detailing either Russell's life or his death, Jane fretted about her kids. She believed they were alive but couldn't understand where they were. Each night, after the Castle closed and Angie shut off the building's many soundtracks and the employees all went home, Jane would stomp through the silent rooms for hours, calling their names. Backstage, lying on his twelve-dollar air mattress between the washing machine and the costume rack, Russell would stuff toilet paper into his ears, squeeze his eyes shut, and imagine himself thousands of miles from Breakneck Beach, riding the gondolas with Claire.

And when Jane's carrying on became insufferable, he would track her down and remind her what everyone else already knew from reading the paper: her kids were living in Piscataway with her sister and brother-in-law. They were well cared for. Usually, this news quieted her down long enough for Russell to return to his mattress for a couple hours of sleep before her frantic searching would begin all over again.

Lizzie Borden, a.k.a. Stacey Nowicki, paused from eating her meatball sub. "Some of us are going out after work. Feel like coming along?"

Russell and Stacey ate lunch together sometimes. Russell would go out to the midway for sandwiches or pizza, and the two of them would eat at the picnic table behind the Castle. Stacey was a theater major at Jersey Central College with unrealistic dreams of starring on Broadway. This was the first time she or anyone else at the Castle had invited him anywhere.

"Where to?" he asked. Today was Sunday, and the park closed early.

"County fair. It'll be a hoot."

"Stacey, we work at an amusement park. It'll be the same as being here."

"We *work* here. There, we'll hang out. Eat funnel cake. Go on some rides. They've got one of those salt-and-pepper—"

"Thanks," he said, "but no." A county fair was about the last place he wanted to go.

"Why not?" She grinned. "Are you afraid of the rides? Is big Russell a chicken?"

"That isn't it."

"Then tell me why."

It was easy to dismiss Stacey as immature. The cigarettes hadn't taken a toll on her voice yet, and with the wig off and her actual hair short and stylish, she certainly looked young, even with the ghoulish makeup. But he hadn't forgotten how she'd soothed those kids earlier in the summer, how steady and reassuring she'd been. He decided to trust her.

"I can't stand watching all those families having a good time," he said. "I used to. But when I look at them now, all I can see is the mess in their future. I see the father in the hospital, or the mother in the morgue."

She put down her meatball sub.

"Is this about that woman who died?" she asked.

"You could say that. Look, Stacey, it's really not worth talking about."

"Oh, I see—you're the strong silent type, is that it?"

He smiled. "I guess you could say that."

She picked up her sandwich again. "Well, maybe don't be a type. Maybe just be a guy." She chewed on her sandwich contemplatively. "One thing's for sure, you need to get away from this place."

He did the opposite, choosing to avoid the midway entirely during the day. The sight no longer gave him any happiness—all those families only made him claustrophobic. The smells burned his nose. The light stung his eyes. Nobody asked him along on any other outings, and Stacey started to eat her lunches with a twerp named Lizard who was always bragging to everybody about what a great bassist he was.

Preferring the Castle's darkness, Russell began to work extra hours without pay. He'd spend nights in the Castle or, when he couldn't sleep, walking the desolate pier. It wasn't the summer job he had imagined, and when Labor Day approached he should have been glad to leave. But where would he go? On Tuesday the park would close for the season, and he hadn't done one damn thing to line up a new job or home.

So when Jane forced him out of bed with her moaning one morning at four a.m., he tracked her down in the Wicked War Room, shook her by the shoulders—she was a lot more solid these days—and yelled: "For God sakes, Jane, shut the fuck up already! Your stupid kids aren't here!"

There were a thousand nicer ways to have said that, but he was feeling the panic of having no options and hoping that a rare night's sleep might spark some ideas.

"Then where are they?" she yelled back. "I demand you tell me!"

They'd been through this so many times. Russell would say "out there," pointing to the world beyond the Castle, and Jane would think he was pointing to the far end of the room and rush over there only to be disappointed all over again.

"I can't explain it to you," he said now, exhausted. "They're out in the world."

She glared at him. "This *is* the world, dummy."

He was about to correct her when he realized she had a point. Other than for groceries, when was the last time he'd gone beyond Happy Land's main gate? The season was over; it was time to leave. But then who would talk Jane down from her terror each night? And who would she bully around?

When Angie arrived several hours later, he asked to speak with her alone in her office. Then he asked if he could stay.

"I don't know, Russ," she said. "I mean, the place will be barren. And I know I'm no Freud, but maybe you shouldn't be living at the scene of the crime any longer. You don't look so hot these days."

He figured as much. The actors seemed to be avoiding him, and they didn't spook easily.

"It's just that I'm going to try to get a job at Bazookas, and I can bike there from here." He shrugged. "Besides—"

"I know," she said. "Free security."

He had no intention of working at Bazookas. He would stay right here, in the Castle with Jane. He owed it to her. He had taken her life, taken her away from her kids, and the least he could do was keep her company until she killed him back.

There was no opportunity to tell Jane his plans until late that evening, when the Labor Day crowd had thinned and they could be alone in the Texas Chainsaw room.

"Listen," he said, "If I were to stay here with you after everyone else was gone for the season, would you want that?"

She looked down at her canvas shoes. "Do whatever you want. It doesn't matter to me one way or the other."

"Okay," he said. "Then I'm going to do it. I'm staying right here. It's you and me."

She looked up at him. "Seriously? You'd do that?"

He thought about his old boss shooting him with a finger

and saying, "Detachment!" But his boss had never killed anybody. And leaving would be like killing her a second time, only worse, because the suffering would go on and on.

"It's done," he said.

She made three lightening-fast loops around the dinner table while the sadists and their captive screamed madly. Then she came back over to Russell looking sad again.

"How long exactly are you planning to stick around?" she asked.

"As long as it takes." It couldn't be long. Jane was much better now at handling the props—they rarely melted through her hands anymore—and it was only a matter of time, he figured, until she got hold of an actual weapon. He'd even caught her the other day with a cigarette lighter she'd lifted from one of the patrons. She couldn't get the flame going. *Smokey the Bear had better be on guard*, he'd joked, trying to keep things light. But the point was, she'd get him eventually.

Which was why it surprised him, just a day later, when the woman so hell-bent on killing him made so basic a mistake. Every morning, he walked to the Sandy Soda for provisions—coffee, beer, microwavable lunches—as soon as the main gate unlocked at 8:55 a.m. Granted, Tuesday was the beginning of the off-season, and at 8:55 the gate remained locked. He'd had to scale the fence to leave the pier. Still, she should have known he'd be out running his errand.

Such a basic mistake, he was thinking as he stood in front of the Sandy Soda with his bag of groceries, watching the first plumes of black smoke rise above the Castle. Like Russell, she had apparently screwed up. Like him, a simple miscalculation meant the difference between life and death.

The Breakneck Beach pier fire would briefly make national

news, the five-acre conflagration burning totally out of control, fueled by gas lines that ran underneath the pier and powered all the restaurants, the rides, the arcades, the Castle of Horrors, and everything else in Happy Land. The wooden pier jutted hundreds of feet into the Atlantic, and the winds that September afternoon blew at gale force, rendering useless the drifting Coast Guard boats and their puny hoses. There would be nothing to do but let the pier consume itself. After thirty years, the pier and everything on it would vanish in just a few short hours, plucked like a bad tooth from the mouth of the Jersey Shore.

Russell stood in front of the Sandy Soda, a block away from Happy Land, as fire trucks and police cars and ambulances began to congregate at the base of the pier. The flames rose higher against the kind of sky that New Jersey saw maybe five days a year—a sky without haze, the blue so deep and rich you want to eat it. The wind was cool, autumn-like, and blew the smoke up and over the water. There was no soot where Russell stood. Instead, the air held traces of fall fish—striped bass, weakfish—that were migrating down from the waters off New England. Russell sniffed the air and wondered where it might blow him tonight when it was time to find a bed.

The first news vans arrived, stopping in the Sandy Soda parking lot. Crowds were gathering. Cameramen shot tape and reporters interviewed onlookers. Then one of the TV reporters and her cameraman approached Russell. The reporter was tall and suspiciously pretty, the first one to get killed off in any slasher flick. It surprised him when she came over and said, "Russell?"

"That's me," he said, and tried to place her. She didn't look like any girl he knew, though any girl he knew would almost certainly be unrecognizable in broad daylight.

She smiled. "Becky Rossi? Breakneck Beach High?"

The name rang a bell, but not the face and definitely not

the body.

Becky held out her hand to shake. "I do this now—you know, TV news?"

"I don't have a TV," he said, shaking her hand. "But I totally believe you."

She asked if he minded being interviewed.

"Sure," he said. "Okay." The cameraman positioned them so that the pier fire made the perfect backdrop.

"You might want to put your groceries down first," Becky said, and he did. "So do you still live in town?"

Russell shrugged. "You could say that."

When the taping started, Becky introduced him as "long-time local." Then she said, "Can I ask you what the Breakneck Beach Pier has meant to you over the years?"

He turned to watch the blaze. The Castle was engulfed in flame. The pier was going fast, and he thought about Jane and wondered what was going to happen to her. Could a dead person burn to death? Would she go homeless? Find her kids? He hoped the pier's destruction might ease her suffering, especially if she believed he was inside. He faced the reporter again. "Mainly it's meant heartache and sadness. I'm pretty relieved to see it go."

"Oh." She signaled for her cameraman to stop taping. When he lowered the camera, she said, "I don't think we're going to use that."

"Sorry," he said. "I don't get interviewed too often." He wished he'd shaved. It'd been a while. At least his clothes were clean. Still, he wished he looked better. She was awfully pretty, and he could imagine getting his heart crushed by her. "Listen," he said, "so if I were to ask you to go bowling with me tonight—you know, like on a date—would you do it?"

She glanced over to the fire. "I've got a big story to cover. It could take a while."

"I know…but after?"

She frowned. "Probably not."

"Oh." It was tempting to leave it at that, end the conversation, which was what security guards did. They said a word or two and then crossed their big arms and watched to be sure there was no trouble. "So you don't bowl?" he asked.

She cocked an eyebrow. "Well, sure I do. I'm actually really…wait, you *know* this, Russell." He must have had a confused expression, because she added, "Um, we were on the *bowling* team together?"

So that's where he knew her. His four weeks of high-school athletics, before getting kicked off the team for buying beer at the bowling alley's bar. He recalled a quiet girl with frizzy hair and an overstuffed backpack. She had seemed smart, but not like someone who needed to brag about her achievements on a t-shirt. And he remembered one other amazing thing.

"You nailed a 7-10 split in practice one time, didn't you?"

She smiled. "Oh, *now* he remembers."

They stood there and watched the Castle's roof cave in. The cameraman scurried closer to the pier for a better shot, but Becky lagged behind, and it felt almost as if Jane, despite everything, had arranged this exact moment—for him to be standing in the Sandy Soda parking lot, saying to this reporter named Becky Rossi whose hair was whipping in the wind, "Come on—two games. I'll even spring for hotdogs."

Becky looked toward the pier, then back at him. "The thing is, I live in Hoboken now." She opened her purse and got out a pen and notepad. "Why don't you try calling me at my mom's house later. She still lives in town. And if I'm still around tonight. . . ."

Soaring high above the old pier, the ghost of Jane Elizabeth Tanner watched the present burn brightly into the future.

Two Truths and a Lie

S o in walks my composition teacher on day one wearing
Levi's 501s and a tweed blazer. Blue collared shirt
unbuttoned just enough for the orange N-C-E of his
PRINCETON t-shirt to peek through. His hair is messy,
intentionally so. I'm around guys quite a bit, what with my
boyfriend being the president of Phi Delta Mu, and I know
what real scruffiness is all about. This isn't it. He tosses his
briefcase on the desk and studies us for a moment, running
his fingers through his hair, and I want to pat him on the
shoulder and tell him to drop the act. It's the 90s, not the
60s. This is no peace rally. All the contrived nonchalance in
the world isn't going to change who he is, an adjunct
instructor who needs to wear his credentials on his t-shirt,
nor will it change who we are: the unimpressed, the hung-
over, products of the public school system, dull and
unmotivated as cows, heads down and grazing our way
toward graduation from Jersey Central College.

He scribbles his name on the chalkboard—Buddy
Munson—then asks us to move our chairs into a circle,
because at some point someone must have told him that
rows are for dictators, while in a circle everybody has an
equal voice. This is obviously bullshit. You throw my family

139

in a circle, my mother will still rule the roost. She'll still make my father feel like shit for losing all that money in Atlantic City, and she'll continue to remind me at every opportunity that my best and only hope is to marry Richy Rich. That's what she calls him, though his real name is John. Short for Jonathan Alexander Garwood III. John's father owns a chain of mattress stores, but he's an older man, past sixty, and John would have to commit some major felonies not to be running the family business in five years.

In order to become acquainted, Buddy has us play a game where we each have to tell two truths about ourselves and one lie. The class will guess which is the lie. By the end of the game, we're supposed to have bonded. As if before taking on such colossal matters as *Writing the Personal Narrative* and *Understanding Academic Discourse*, it's vital to know that Sheila, for instance, got knocked up at prom, or rides a Harley.

I'm the only senior in a class of dopey freshman. For four years I've put off this requirement on account of how stupid it is. So now that I'm just nine credits shy of a degree in psychology, I've got to take a class aimed at teaching me how to write a college paper. Total waste of time, and all I can hope for is entertainment value. But the freshmen don't even understand how Buddy's game is meant to be played, that the idea is to tell *interesting* things about yourself. The first kid, a fat boy who squints, goes, "I'm left-handed. I'm from Cleveland. I wear contact lenses."

Buddy sighs. "So which do you suppose is the lie?" The game goes on, each kid telling truths that could be lies and lies that could be truths—*I'm majoring in business, I have two brothers, I play the tenor saxophone, my birthday is in June, I ate Chinese food last weekend*—but we're not learning a damn thing of substance about anyone.

When it gets to my turn, I tell three lies. I look around

the circle of my classmates and say, "I've had three abortions. I stole my mother's wedding ring last summer to buy crystal meth. I have an ashtray fetish and love to lick out the ashes." I saw that in a documentary in my Abnormal Psych class.

It's a brilliant moment. The kids don't know what to say. I can almost hear their brains groaning to a start, like metal on metal. Buddy winks in my direction, so either he's hip to me or hitting on me, and frankly either one will make the semester a little livelier.

"Maybe you should just tell us," one of the girls says. Chickenshit.

I go, "Maybe you should guess." But when nobody does, I tell the class that the lie was having had three abortions. I fold my hands on my desk and smirk. "I've only had *two* abortions."

I could have gone with the ashtray licking. What matters is they believe the wedding ring story to be true. It'll keep class interesting. I like the idea of these kids checking their pockets and the zippers on their backpacks, counting and recounting the cash in their wallets.

When we're done with the game, class is nearly over. Before dismissing us, Buddy tells us to write a short story for next Monday. Any topic. Five pages.

All the freshmen start moaning, but I'm thinking: piece of cake. I'll turn in the same story I wrote last year for my creative writing class. Father loses life savings at the blackjack table while devoted family thinks he's putting in overtime at the tire factory. Bankruptcy ensues. Family sells house, moves to a dreary rental on the business loop. Son shaves head, joins the Marines. Daughter foregoes dreams of a college that actually rejects some of its applicants. Begins dating fraternity brother, spends all her time at the frat house. Drinks too much beer and vodka one night, lands in the hospital, nearly dies.

"But what do we write about?" some girl asks.

Buddy says, "Only two stories have ever been written."
Then he writes on the board:

1) A stranger comes to town

2) A person travels to a strange and unfamiliar place

"Every story," he says, "is some variation on these two themes." He nods like he's just said something important, but I'm thinking he's wrong. In my story—hell, in my life—where's the stranger? The only stranger I've met lately is him, the instructor, and he doesn't carry anywhere near the sense of menace or mystery that a word like *stranger* evokes. And as for an unfamiliar place, nothing is remotely unfamiliar about the damn Central College, where as a child I took ballet lessons, and piano lessons, and karate, a school that ever since I can remember has hocked itself on Sunday afternoon television:

Your own future, your own Central College,
A place for fun, a place for knowledge.

I'm convinced that Buddy is way off-base—only two stories, yeah right—until twenty minutes later when I arrive at the Phi Delta Mu house to find somebody I've never seen before up on a ladder, scrubbing the windows over the front door. He's older than I am, but not *old.* Buddy's age, maybe, and rail thin. His pants are tattered and too short, and his canvas sneakers are coming apart. Even though it's January in Jersey, the guy's face is shiny with sweat from working hard. His shirt could be wrung out.

As I come closer to the ladder his scrubbing speeds up (all men are show-offs), and some of his greasy sweat lands on the stoop beside me. Is this my stranger? It would figure. "Hey"—I look up and point at him—"watch where you're dripping."

He glances down and mutters, "Sorry." He's got green eyes and isn't bad looking in a stray-dog, underfed kind of way, and from the way he avoids my gaze, I believe he *is* sorry. As I leave him to go inside, he starts scrubbing like a madman.

In the frat house, John and his buddies have cleared out all the furniture and the foosball table and the projection TV from the common room and are setting up the boxing ring.

"Who's the stranger outside?" I ask.

"His name's Gunnipuddy," John says, tugging the ropes tight around the ring.

"Well, that's a stupid name." Because I'd rather my stranger have a name like Hank or Rusty.

"Get used to it," he says. "He's our new maintenance man."

By maintenance man, he means janitor. He means toilet scrubber. Puke mopper. And it's about time. It's only been a week since the old maintenance man quit without warning to buy an RV and retire in Georgia, but the brothers aren't the sort to pitch in when it comes to cleaning, and the house is filthy even for itself.

My stranger doesn't know it yet because it's only his first day, but cleaning the windows is going to feel like a day off compared to cleaning the house after a Phi Delta Mu party. And in just two nights the frat house will be crammed with hundreds of drunk and stoned undergrads, each having paid twenty bucks to enter the boxing pool. Sixteen contestants— all frat brothers—will face off in a single-elimination tournament of one-round bouts. By the end of the night, one boxer will be named champion, whoever has bet on him will win half the cash, and the other half will go to the fraternity's chosen charity, breast cancer awareness.

Boxing Night might not seem like the wisest event for a fraternity that's perennially on the brink of losing its charter, but it's become a significant university tradition and the biggest fundraiser on Greek Street. Everybody knows that on the first Friday night of spring semester, you come to

Phi Delta Mu and put down your twenty bucks and catch some live boxing action. And in nearly a decade, nobody has gotten too badly injured. Banged-up, sure. Bloodied, sure. But the fighters are all friends, more or less, and they all wear mouthpieces and headgear and groin protectors. Anyway, the guys love their cuts and bruises, because they are battle scars that can be shown off long after the event is over.

John is favored to win. His payout is a meager three-to-one. For weeks the guys have sat around at night, setting and re-setting odds. The same guys who flunked trig have suddenly become as skillful as actuaries, creating probability tables on their computers, arguing late into the night about setting lines and spreading risks. Most of the boxers come in at five-to-one, seven-to-one, ten-to-one. The long shot is a kid in my psych classes, Leon, who is short and bow-legged and possibly asthmatic, and who gets so excited when telling you about hallucinatory mushrooms that spit collects on his upper lip. Leon is paying fifty-to-one.

Dozens of students, maybe even hundreds of them, have already paid their twenty bucks. I've bet on John, of course, and will jump around like wild for him publicly, but I also placed twenty on Leon because, hell, I could use five hundred bucks.

At lunch, when I tell John about playing Two Truths and a Lie in my composition class, he doesn't get how funny it was. He swallows the last of his meatball sub and goes, "You seem pretty hung up on this teacher. Are you *into* this guy?"

Oh, and John can get jealous for no reason at all. Have I described Buddy as attractive? As tempting? Just the opposite. He is the worst sort of dork—the sort that pretends not to be.

"Trust me," I tell him. "When I decide to make a man out of Buddy boy, you'll be the first to know."

A few laughs escape from the next table. We're in the tap room of Phi Delta Mu, and at noon the tables are occupied by big beefy guys eating big beefy lunches. John doesn't like the brothers knowing we have a relationship where I can bust his balls in good fun. Or maybe we don't actually have that sort of relationship. John has a lot going for him—amazing body, relief pitcher on the baseball team—but his sense of humor is lacking. I've explained this to my mother, but her sense of humor is lacking, too. Anyway, I've never minded a jealous boyfriend.

At least he's predictable. *That* I like. He'll put hot sauce on his three hardboiled eggs every day till he dies. You'll find him opening night at any new Steven Seagal movie, and on nights when we've been drinking, he'll always force me to down two tall glasses of water before going to bed. He'll rub my shoulders after I've taken a hard exam. He'll buy me a dozen red roses on Valentine's Day. And most importantly, he will *not* stupidly put at risk everything that is supposedly important to him. John and I aren't perfect together—maybe from time to time I ask myself if this is all there is—but at least I know what I'm dealing with.

John gets up from the table with his protein shake (he's off beer until after Boxing Night), goes over to the jukebox, and starts flipping through the song list. Screaming guitars begin to play. Metallica, I think. The jukebox is filled with songs that make you want to conquer weaker people. John stands there facing it for a moment, nodding in time with the beat. Then he's back at our table again, scooping up our drinks. "Come on."

I get up and follow him. "Where are we going?" I ask, though with a coy lilt because I know exactly where we're going. John leads me through the house, to the staircase. One of the brothers, coming down the stairs, goes, "Be careful, Garwood. That's bad luck before a fight."

"Fight isn't until Friday," John says, and punches the other guy on the shoulder as we pass.

As president of the fraternity, John has the largest bedroom, up on the third floor, overlooking the soccer fields. The first time he led me up here during a party was pretty exciting. It still is. Spring nights, the breeze blows in and chills our sweaty bodies, and mornings I wake up to the sweet, yeasty smell from the bread factory a mile away. Spring isn't for a few months yet, but this afternoon is warm enough to use John's clanky fan, which he keeps on a milk crate by the bed. It's a terrific bed, queen-sized mattress, a million springs, courtesy of his dad. John and I both have 1:30 classes, but we can fit a lot of activity into an hour.

After my dad lost all that money, the whole family started going to see Herve, our therapist. This was before I started college and decided to major in psychology and came to understand that Herve had been practicing his own brand of Client-Centered Therapy, originally developed by Carl Rogers in the 1950s. I didn't understand that by having us remove our shoes and by playing George Benson CDs in the background, Herve was creating a "growth-promoting climate," and that by parroting back everything we said with a voice so calm you wanted to elbow him in the teeth, he was showing respect for our feelings and expressing "unconditional positive regard." I also didn't know that Client-Centered Therapy was almost completely out of favor by then, except with therapists who were lazy or hippied-out or both. I just thought, considering what we were paying him, that he ought to do more than repeat all of our bullshit back to us.

That was on Monday nights. On Thursdays we went to a support group where other dads and moms whined about gambling away their life savings. We met in the private room at the rear of Ino's Pizza, so that Ino, first-generation

American and Lotto addict, could dart back and forth between the meeting and the kitchen.

The room throbbed with fear and desperation. Voices quavered. Sobs arose from nowhere. They were a sorry lot, these people, and I felt that my own family was far superior to them. My dad wasn't violent or even an asshole. He had coached my softball team in the sixth through eighth grades. In high school, he had done my chemistry homework for me. He hadn't ever imposed a curfew on me or my brother, Paul. All he did wrong was lose a lot of money. We had to move out of the house. We had to sell a car and some jewelry. Still, aren't we taught that money isn't everything? That it's the root of all evil? So there you go, I remember thinking. My dad might have screwed up, but he had cleansed my family's souls in the process.

Mom didn't regard Dad as any soul-cleanser. Used to be, Mom would always laugh at Dad's corny puns. His goofy charm made her smile. Not anymore. Frown lines formed around her mouth. Her eyes darkened a shade. Then again, it was mostly her money that Dad had lost, inheritance from her parents.

I'm making it sound as if I was completely accepting of my dad's vice. Not so, apparently. Because when it was my turn to speak, I stood and told the group gathered at Ino's Pizza that I'd give ten dollars to whoever could guess what color panties I was wearing. "Come on, people," I said, walking around the room like I owned it. "What's the matter with you? I'm paying out ten bucks here. Where else are you going to get something for nothing?"

Dad sucked his teeth. Mom shot me a murderous glance. The air was heavy, I remember, everyone snickering and sighing and whatnot, though some of them, I'll bet, were itching to guess a color. My brother took me by the arm and led me outside behind Ino's. We lit up cigarettes, and I laughed until I cried, and Paul skipped the laughing part and went straight to crying, and he told me how lucky I was to be leaving for college in half a year, and I said I wasn't going anywhere, dummy, because there wasn't any money for that anymore, and he said that he was thinking of joining the Marines or something so that he could get out of the house, which he did.

I get home in the late afternoon as the sun is coming down over the Ford dealership across the street. I shove open the front door because it doesn't sit right in the door frame. Nothing in this rental house works the way it's supposed to. But when we moved, Mom and Dad said *no apartment*—that was where they drew the line— so here we are, the lone residence on the business loop. Two-bedroom house with cracked siding and rusty water and a heater that runs too hot or not at all. Shag rugs that reek of cat piss. Bathtub stained fungus-green. And our neighbors: two parking lots.

I dig around my bedroom closet for my box of old schoolwork. The story I wrote last year for my creative writing class was called "Betting It All." The facts I included were essentially true, but I skipped over the parts that made me look bad. For instance, I avoided everything about therapy and the support group. I included the part about my spending the night in the hospital, because my story needed a climax. But mainly it was just a lot of preachy nonsense about how Mom's behavior toward my dad was just as lousy, in its own way, as his own behavior had been, and how the daughter got psychologically screwed in the end, embittered and unable to trust another human being. Rereading it now, I know I won't hand it in again. The story is melodramatic and whiny. Undoubtedly it got an "A" not because the teacher found it insightful or clever or because of its refreshing turns of phrase, but because the punctuation and spelling checked out, which, at Central

College, a place for fun and a place for knowledge, is the best that our teachers can hope for.

But also, I feel done with this particular family drama. Beyond it. Four years since we sold the house, and Mom hasn't eased up at all. Last month my dad fell on the ice in the parking lot at work, and ever since, Mom has been calling him Klutz and Screw-up. But if she wants to keep torturing him for past failures, and if he's okay with the arrangement, then who am I to pass judgment? In June I'll be done with Central College, and I swear you'll hear the sound of rubber meeting road. You'll see me not looking back. Maybe John will come with me wherever it is I go, but whenever I picture the open highway, my only companion is a box of mix tapes.

I decide to write a new story for Monday, one that looks to the future rather than the past, about a woman who starts a new life by making off with a stolen sports car, an Alfa Romeo spider convertible, and she drives west from Jersey to California, robbing banks and evading the law and breaking stereotypes and hearts.

I tear a blank sheet of paper out of my notebook and lean back in my chair, thinking about how my heroine will steal that car. When I hear my parents shove open the front door, I get up to say hello and maybe get some cookies from the pantry to help me to think better. Seeing them, I stop in my tracks.

I need to back up.

Ever since I was a kid, Dad worked in the accounting department at the tire factory. But after the whole losing-the-house incident, Mom quit her job in real estate and started working there, too—right in Dad's department, to keep an eye on him. (At the time, Herve suggested that maybe Mom had overstepped some boundary. Maybe she ought to trust Dad a little more than that. That was when we stopped seeing Herve.)

So when Dad fell on the ice last month outside the factory

and broke his wrist, Mom told me—with characteristic empathy—that she'd witnessed firsthand his "latest display of grace." When they got home from the hospital, I found a magic marker in the kitchen drawer and signed my name, Alice, on the cast they'd put over his hand, and I drew a heart over the "i."

When I tried to hand Mom the marker, she said, "Forget it. I might write something I'll regret."

Cruel, but typical. What I'm getting at is that I thought my family had come to work as follows:

A) Four years ago, Dad lost a lot of money

B) Ever since, Mom has made Dad pay, which was unfair because

C) What was in the past was in the past

What I see in the doorway, however, changes everything. Mom is carrying Dad's suit jacket and white button-down shirt and tie. Dad's got on just his dress pants and a white undershirt. His right arm is still in a cast. But now his *left* arm—which for the past month he's been forced to drive with and eat with and do everything else with—now *it's* in a cast, too. The new cast goes up past his elbow and is hanging in a sling. For a second I think he really *is* a klutz. But the weather has been so warm, there isn't any ice to slip on. He's standing there with the strangest look on his face—an embarrassed grin, if I had to name it—when suddenly the answer comes to me, like it must for a detective or a codebreaker. Dad didn't fall again. He never fell in the first place. Which means that I've completely missed D:

D) Daughter is an idiot

Seeing him standing there with two casts is almost comical. Almost. Because you get casts put on when your bones are broken, and if dad hasn't been breaking his own bones, then we've entered a world where people are breaking them for him. It's the world of mobster movies. This is hard for me to get my head around. My dad works in a tire factory. He wears a tie and sits at a computer all day long. He understands chemistry and cooks a good bacon and potato soup.

"I want the truth from you," I tell him. "So start talking."

Mom goes, "Take it easy on him, Al. Your father fell."

"He fell? I'd like to know how he fell!" I'm feeling hysterical. "Tell me exactly how he fell!"

"What do you mean, how? Your father fell down. And you're being very loud."

"*Tell me how!*" I scream. When my dad winces, I lower my voice and say to him, "Or maybe you'll tell me the truth. That somebody. . .*did* this to you."

We stand there for a minute while Dad decides what to do. Then he says, "This is part of life, too."

If his words were meant to be wise or somehow comforting, they aren't. "I'm going to be sick," I announce.

I'm not being dramatic. I run to the bathroom, kneel by the toilet, and get sick. When I feel like I won't puke anymore, I flush the toilet, then move the clothes that Mom has soaking in the sink over to the bathtub so I can rinse out my mouth and brush my teeth. My mom opens the door and comes into the bathroom.

"Are you all right?" she asks as I'm spitting toothpaste. As usual, shirts and pants and underwear are hanging up all over the bathroom, drying. For a while we had a clothes line out back, but people kept stealing our things.

"You lied to me," I tell her. "I thought you were being such an asshole."

"We didn't want you involved," she says.

"And *him*," I say, loud enough for my dad to hear. "He needs help. He needs a whole goddamn team."

"Actually," he calls from the other room, "I need money. Come here, honey, let me get you a glass of water."

But I don't want anything from anybody, so I leave the bathroom and walk straight out the front door and away from the house, which I immediately regret because it's gotten really cold outside. Sure enough, a few seconds later my dad is hurrying after me with my coat.

"How could you keep gambling after losing our house?" I ask him after putting the coat on. "What the hell were you thinking?"

I don't expect an answer. I don't get one. We walk in silence along the small perimeter of slushy dead grass bordering our rental property, and once we've completed a loop we head to one of the parking lots, which this time of day is mostly empty. I want my dad to cry. I'm not sure I've ever seen him cry before, and right now would be a good time. I want him to crave my pity, to need it as much as he needs to play craps or poker or bet on the Rangers or whatever he does.

Finally he stops walking and rests his right arm, heavy from the cast, on my shoulder. He's looking out across the road, where the lights from the car dealerships glow a misty orange. "Sometimes, honey, I have this fantasy where I win enough money to fix all the problems I've ever caused. I buy your mother an even bigger house than the one we had. A better house. And things are so good."

"Dad."

"Alice, listen to me a minute." Now he's looking at me. "We have a butler. A private chef. A three-car garage. And I buy you the nicest jewelry you ever saw. A pearl necklace and diamond earrings. And your brother, when he comes home on leave, there's a Porsche parked in the driveway waiting for him."

As he shares this fairy tale, it dawns on me how naïve I've been, thinking all this time that losing our stupid house was *the* event, *the* towering symbol of how out-of-hand things have gotten. Losing the house always felt like rock bottom. *My dad lost our house*, I told John on our second date, a fact that felt important and shocking when I said it. *My dad lost our house*, I told my friends at the moment when I most desired their deepest pity. But now it seems that losing the house was just a rung down a ladder to some subterranean place I've never even considered. There's still a wife to lose, isn't there? And friends. A career. Me and Paul. There's still money to be borrowed and lost, and then more money, and when he can't repay it there are still other bones to break. And after he's been humiliated and broken and crushed for long enough, after he's lost everything and *still* craves the action, there's a bed in the middle of the afternoon on which he can sit and put the end of a gun to his temple or in his mouth, and he can weigh the relief that would come from pulling the trigger against the image of me and Paul and Mom in a funeral home, looking at his closed casket because of what he's done to himself. And *that*—sitting on that bed and making that sort of decision—is what you call rock bottom. Until then, Dad isn't done yet. This thing hasn't run its course. Not by a long shot.

I also should have known from being a psych major, as well as a human being, that people don't change without really wanting to. And even if you do want to change, the odds are strongly against you. No addict worth a lick would ever bet on his own recovery. It's like Newton's Law, how once you're already in motion you tend to keep going the way you're going. Dad will always feel the tug of beating the odds, and John will always be the favorite, and people like my stranger Gunnipuddy will always be cleaning other people's toilets.

My dad is still going on and on about his stupid fantasy, so I tell him to shut up already. Then I ask, "Is your score settled now? Now that they've broken your arm?"

"Wrist, honey. Just the wrist." He's trying to be funny. When he sees it's not working, he lifts his arm off my shoulder and looks at me. "I'm afraid it doesn't work that way."

"You mean you still owe it?"

He nods.

"Can't Mom pay it?"

"She doesn't have that kind of cash."

"What kind of cash?"

He shrugs. "Fifteen thousand."

"Jesus, Dad, you're in some real trouble."

His laugh can probably be heard all the way across the parking lot. It's a dark, angry sound, unlike any I can remember my father making before.

Because it's the first week of classes and nobody's got any real work to do, practically the whole fraternity is hanging out in the common room. Guys are making use of the boxing ring, jumping around, tackling each other. A few have gloves on and are sparring. They all love it, you can tell. That boxing ring fulfills a thousand childhood fantasies of being strong, being the center of attention, being all-American. Every guy in the place seems to have invited his girlfriend over tonight, and you'd think it was a scheduled party, so many people are hanging out drinking and smoking cigarettes and shouting. Even Leon the long shot is in the ring. Getting used to the feel of things. He looks detached from the scene, though, as if watching wild animals on a nature show. Seeing me, he calls out, "Hey, Alice, how about you and me go a few rounds right now?"

He's kidding, but I'm tempted to take him up on it because I feel ready to punch somebody. "Where's John?"

"The gym. I swear, he's taking this too seriously." And then with an *oof!* Leon gets sacked to the mat by Roy, who played offensive line in high school and is twice Leon's size.

I go to the tap room, pour a beer, and take it upstairs to John's room. I lie in his bed and think about my dad as he stood there in the doorway, wearing two casts, a pained and embarrassed grin on his face. I think about hunting down my brother, because this seems like the sort of crisis he ought to know about. But you can't just dial him up in East Timor. You have to send a letter, and he won't get it for weeks. So I focus on the more urgent matter of how the hell you get your hands on fifteen thousand dollars.

Even though John's family is rich, I can't ask him for that kind of money. I just can't. But a five-hundred-dollar bet on Leon at fifty-to-one, split evenly with the breast cancer people, would still give Dad close to what he needs. It's a gamble. And super ironic, gambling to save the gambler. Other thoughts swirl in my head, too, like the fact that my father is out of his fucking mind, and that even if he pays off this particular debt he still won't have learned his lesson. But it's all about priorities. And the first priority is to stop whoever keeps breaking my dad's bones from breaking any more of them.

When John gets home I put off what I know I have to do, and not until morning do I finally ask him for the money. It's hard, asking him, because I'm very particular about being independent and self-reliant, etc., and it's even harder telling him, when he asks what I need the cash for, that it isn't any of his business. I'm not trying to be rude or distant with John. But he isn't family, just my boyfriend. I'd always told him that my dad's gambling problems were ancient history. Now I feel ashamed not only for my dad, but for myself, for believing that a handful of sessions with Herve and a few months at Ino's Pizza magically cured him.

John is brushing his hair in front of the mirror. When I ask him to lend me five hundred dollars, he sits down on the bed. "You're pregnant," he says.

I deny it, and he doesn't press the matter. He just says okay and squeezes my shoulder and goes sort of pale. He assumes I'm pregnant and not telling him the truth, and that I'll deal with it on my own.

Leon never should have entered the match. He can't weigh more than 130 pounds, and you can tell from the spazzy way he plays pool or foosball that he was picked last for any number of teams growing up. So it's hardly a surprise when, just hours before the event is to begin, he chickens out.

He explains with great passion—tears are in his eyes—that he won't fight his own brothers, even for a cause as worthy as breast cancer awareness. Nothing to do with being afraid, he says. "Hell, I'll take a beating if that's what needs to happen. But the brother-against-brother thing. I just can't abide it, morally."

Nobody believes him for a second. Leon, like all the rest, was walking around campus all week with visions of being a champion. But after standing in the ring and watching the others spar, he has come to understand that his fifty-to-one odds are, if anything, extremely generous.

"People have already bet on you!" John tells him. "Lots of people. You can't drop out now."

"Sorry, guys," Leon says. "I'm out."

"Well, shit." John looks at me. "Where are we going to find another fifty-to-one shot?"

Dozens of heads swivel in unison toward the new maintenance man, who has just come around the corner into the common room holding a broom and dustpan.

"Forget it," says Rick, one of the odds-makers. "That man is no fifty-to-one shot."

"Hey, G.," John says, "how tall are you? Six feet?"

"Six one," Gunnipuddy says.

"What do you weigh? Two bills?"

"Less."

"Ever box before?"

"No."

"See?" John says to Rick. "Man's never boxed before." Then he explains to Gunnipuddy about Leon dropping out of the match. "We need a replacement. You're it."

Gunnipuddy looks at the ring again. "Nah, I don't think so. You guys look pretty serious about this, and I'm no fighter."

"Come on, big guy," Leon says, now that his replacement is in sight. "It's for charity. And it'd really be helping us out. It'd really show your commitment to—"

"No fucking way," I tell the room. "He said he doesn't want to fight." My own words surprise me, since I have more to gain than anybody by having Gunnipuddy take Leon's place. Betting on Leon, I was throwing my money away. At least Gunnipuddy might stand a chance. Still, I don't like them strong-arming him. These days, straight-up honesty is sitting a lot better with me than strong-armed manipulation. "Gunnipuddy, you don't have to do this. We'll figure something else out."

"Whoa, wait a minute, Alice—maybe he *wants* to fight," John says. "We use soft gloves." He tosses one over. Gunnipuddy catches it and presses it with his thumbs. "See? And we really need you."

Gunnipuddy slides his hand into the glove and punches his other palm a few times. "I won't be any good. I've only ever hit one guy before."

"Well, maybe it's time to hit another," John says. "Anyway, you don't have to be good. You're the long shot."

"And you say you need me to do this?"

"We do," John says. "The fraternity needs you. We're all on the same team here."

If I were Gunnipuddy I'd be pissed at having to listen to such horseshit. The man signed on for janitorial duty, not this. He takes the glove off his hand and tosses it back to John. "Okay."

Suddenly they're all clapping him on the back and making him feel like a million bucks. They put him up on the scale and ask him about himself so they can introduce him properly when it's his turn to fight.

Four hours later the common room is packed with people I've never seen before and people I see all the time, everybody shouting and drinking beer and spilling beer and dancing and hitting on one another and shoving one another and working themselves up for the event. I know John can take care of himself, but I'm worried about my long shot. I need him to win, but I also want him to win. He might be my stranger who waltzes in and saves my family without even knowing it, but from his perspective Phi Delta Mu is the strange place that he's come to visit. I'd like his story to include a victory like this one.

Everybody gathers around the ring and the music shuts off, and one of the brothers, dressed in a tux jacket, bow tie, and blue jeans, welcomes everybody to Boxing Night. He thanks everyone for their contribution to breast cancer awareness and promises a spectacular night of boxing.

And because of the seeding process, where the long shots meet the favorites in the first round, right off the bat Gunnipuddy gets matched up against the man most favored to win. John.

In this corner, the announcer is saying, wearing the brown shorts, hailing from right here in Breakneck Beach, weighing in at 179 pounds, is the challenger, Gunnipuddy. Who, by the way, is looking out at a sea of strangers, pale and afraid.

And in the other corner, wearing blue shorts, stands my boyfriend, whose eyes are as focused as when he's about to throw a pitch, whose protein shakes are looking like they've paid off, and who, it is absolutely clear, is about to pound the hell out of my poor stranger.

In the instant before the bell rings, I have a fantasy where Gunnipuddy wins round after round, defying the odds, culminating in my winning fifteen thousand dollars, which I use to bail my father out of his predicament. My father turns his life around, I graduate summa cum laude and get a high-paying job in California, my mother gets promoted to vice president, she and Dad buy the old house back, and my brother parlays his military career into a successful run in the state Senate. Every long shot comes in. A beautiful fantasy.

Then the bell rings, and people start cheering, and Gunnipuddy actually lands the first punch. There isn't much force behind it, but one of his long arms connects with John's chest. Then John slaughters him.

Gunnipuddy was right—he's no fighter. He arms hang at his sides, useless, and John is landing some fast and hard blows. To the body. To the head. Last year John couldn't enter Boxing Night because of a sprained ankle. Watching him now, I'm impressed with his strength. I really am. But it's also horrifying, watching this guy I've been sleeping with for two years hit another person so hard. "Fall down!" I'm shouting, but Gunnipuddy stands there, arms dangling, staggering but stupidly upright, and only when a punch to the chin sends him spinning does he land on the mat.

Soft padded gloves, my ass. I crawl into the ring and kneel over him. When I touch his face, his eyes open. The idiot is smiling up at me. It's unsettling—his lips are swollen and his eyes are unfocused, plus that head of his keeps bleeding. When I yell for somebody to call 911, it's like that dream when you're yelling something important but nobody can hear you. It's so loud in there that in the end I have to leave Gunnipuddy alone on the mat to call for help myself. The ambulance seems to take forever to arrive, which is just as well since the guys insist on moving Gunnipuddy outside and away from the hundreds of drunk, underage undergrads. So they half carry, half walk him out to the street, and tell the EMTs that they found him out here all smashed up. The EMTs look skeptical, but they strap him to a gurney and carry him away. I'm embarrassed to say, none of us rides with him. He is still a stranger to us.

I sleep in John's bed that night even though I'm angry at him. For what exactly, I'm not sure. Still, I face away from him. "I'm not a bully or anything," John tells me, rubbing my back. "It's boxing. You have to make the other guy go down." I don't say anything. I just lie there looking at the window, where outside it's dark. "We were wearing gloves," he says. His fingers feel soft on my skin. He could have just come from a spa. "Sometimes people get hurt even when you take precautions. It's boxing. Things happen."

In my dream, my parents are murdered and my brother refuses to fly home for the funeral. Then I sleep for a few hours without dreaming. When I awake again it's still very early, but lighter, and all I hear besides the birds outside is the unlikely sound of the downstairs bathroom being cleaned. The digital clock on John's night table reads 7:05 a.m. I slide out of bed and put on a pair of my shorts and a t-shirt that are on the floor, and I go downstairs. The boxing ring is still there, along with countless plastic cups and bottles on tables and the floor and on bookshelves and on the television and every available surface. The house smells sour but is absolutely still except for the sounds coming from the bathroom. I tap on the door and then walk in. Gunnipuddy, bless his heart, is mopping the tile floor.

The bathroom smells industrial and lemony. Gunnipuddy has on blue jeans, a white t-shirt, and his canvas sneakers. His right eye is swollen shut and purple, and there's a bandage taped to his forehead. When he sees me he smiles, then winces, then smiles again, then winces again. This could go on forever, so I say, "You should have slept in. I think the guys would understand."

He looks down and seems intent on getting the stain out of a particular tile, scrubbing back and forth, but I think it's just a flawed tile. "I couldn't sleep. How was the rest of Boxing Night?"

"You sort of put an end to it. If you want to know the truth, the guys were pretty mad at me for calling an ambulance." When Gunnipuddy looks confused, I explain, "They're afraid of getting booted off campus."

"Oh, sorry."

"Don't be. Does your head hurt?"

"Not really," he says. "I'm on some good medicine. I'm okay."

"How many stitches you got under there?"

"I don't know. A few. I keep thinking about last night."

"You're probably better off not thinking about it," I tell him. "I never saw anybody get beat up like that before. It was scary."

"No, not the fight," he says. "I was thinking about . . . I mean, the part where you. . . ."

I know that gaze. He's taken a beating, he's had stitches sewn into him, but I don't want him to think things that are untrue. So I shake my head. "Don't get any ideas. I didn't want you to get killed, is all. Jesus, don't think it meant anything."

Then, feeling like I've been too harsh on the poor sucker only hours after being beaten to a pulp, I make the ultimate sacrifice. I take a scrub brush out of a metal bucket, get down on my hands and knees, and start scrubbing the floor underneath the sinks. Holy shit, don't ever clean the floor of a men's room if you don't have to. Suddenly I understand the value of a college education, even from a lousy place like Central College. Anyway, I'm scrubbing away and trying to think of something to say that won't give Gunnipuddy the wrong idea. "Where did you work," I ask him, "before coming here?"

He seems to like that question, because he whistles and goes, "Oh, I've had lots of jobs. I left Breakneck Beach at fifteen and didn't come back until recently, so I've done about everything." He tells me about bussing tables in Cape May and cleaning office buildings in D.C., and a summer gig he had raking the beaches in Nags Head, North Carolina.

"For a while I cleaned up waste sites. That wasn't such a good job, but it sure paid well. I got a bad cough in my chest and had to quit."

He stopped mopping the floor while he talked to me. Now that he's done talking, he starts mopping again.

"All your jobs involve cleaning up after other people. Do you love trash or something?"

He laughs. "No. But most people don't like it more than I don't like it, which means that there's usually a job for me when I need one."

He passes the mop several times over the world's most putrid section of floor tile. There's no word for the color.

"This place gets pretty disgusting," I tell him. "I guess you're finding that out."

He shrugs. "I like it here. I could stay here a while." It was as if he didn't remember that eight hours earlier he'd been beaten nearly unconscious.

"Even after what happened last night?"

His fingertips move instinctively to the bandage, then down again to the mop. "Look, this might sound dumb to someone like you, but I like how the guys were talking about how everybody was on the same team. You know?"

I *knew* he'd hooked into that line of bullshit, and I'm angry at the brothers for homing in on the guy's loneliness and using it against him. "They didn't mean it," I tell him. "Christ, I'm sorry to break this to you, but they just needed another boxer. You know that, don't you?"

He nods, thinking to himself. "Maybe."

"I mean, some of them aren't bad guys, but they aren't looking for new friends."

"But if I didn't fight, they'd have held it against me for as long as I worked here. That's no way to start a job. Especially a job with good pay, and room and board. I mean, I hope to stay here a long time, you know?"

I smile and say, "Well, I hope you stay a long time, too."

This felt like the right thing to say until the second it was out of my mouth. I immediately recognize it for the mistake it is. Gunnipuddy gives me that intense gaze again, and our nice conversation is derailed.

"You do?"

I shrug, trying to downplay my words. But the shrug feels staged. "Yeah, sure."

Well, no way should I have reaffirmed it. Because suddenly Gunnipuddy is kneeling beside me, right by the urinal, and—whammo!—kissing me on the mouth, and since I'm down on my haunches, I sort of tip over backward and then I'm flat on my ass, on a part of the floor that hasn't been cleaned yet. I get so mad I fling the scrubber at him, but I miss, and it skims across the tile floor and comes to rest by the heating vent.

"God dammit," I say. It actually wasn't a bad kiss. The angle was about right considering how quickly he moved in, and his breath was surprisingly minty. "Didn't I just tell you not to get any ideas?" I stand up. "Are you stupid or something?"

He goes, "Oh, man. I'm so sorry. Oh…" And he gets up and runs—literally runs—out of the bathroom. I follow him, but he's already out the frat's front door, running like police dogs are chasing him. Which makes me sad, because while he shouldn't have done what he did, it wasn't *that* big a deal. What if it was the boldest thing he's ever done? I wouldn't want him to think he should never take a chance or be spontaneous or whatever. For all I know, Gunnipuddy hasn't kissed many girls before, and now I've tainted the whole experience for him.

I hoped that would be the end of it, but a couple of hours later Gunnipuddy goes and, like an idiot, tells John. All I can figure is that in the story that Gunnipuddy tells himself, he's probably noble. As long as you're the hero of your own story, you might as well be a noble hero, right?

I was in John's room trying to phone my parents. Trying, but failing, because ever since my dream last night I've developed this crazy and irrational fear of calling home. But *is* it crazy? *Is* it irrational? I'm afraid of an unfamiliar voice answering the phone and giving me terrible news. I keep dialing six digits, then hanging up. Finally, I give up and head downstairs, and when I get to the TV room, there's John, his forearm up to Gunnipuddy's throat, saying, "I swear I'll make that other eye blacker than the first, you son of a bitch." That's where Gunnipuddy's nobility has gotten him.

"I stepped over the line," Gunnipuddy says. "I know that I did."

"You fucking leapt over it," John tells him, "and now you're gonna pay."

But John isn't a violent guy, just jealous, and overprotective, and sometimes quick to anger. He stares Gunnipuddy down for a long moment, then lowers his arm and storms off to the tap room, not even looking at me. But every other guy in the place sure is.

Monday morning Gunnipuddy packs his belongings into a U-haul. Nobody helps him. The brothers toss a football in the front yard and make him walk around them with his crates and boxes. It's another warm day for January, and mud is getting on his night table and bookshelf, which he drags across the lawn to the truck. To make a show of it, John fixes us stupid-looking drinks. He doesn't know how to mix drinks, so they've got a lot of competing liquors that taste like hell. We sit on the front porch in our coats and John clinks his glass against mine and says, "Cheers," then asks me if I'd like to go with him to Los Cabos for spring break. His treat. He's talking about romantic hikes and surfing lessons and a beachfront suite with a hot tub, and I have this fear that when we're there, he's going to propose.

I want to get in my car and drive away from John and Phi Delta Mu. I want to go home but I'm terrified of what I'll find there. So I sit and watch my stranger get into the U-haul, and I listen to John prattle on about humpback whale watching, and I down my disgusting drink, and I wish to God I were that woman in the stolen sports car heading west. The woman who beats all the odds, blocks every punch, fears nothing. Which reminds me that I never wrote the damn story that's due later today. I'll be handing in the old one after all.

As Gunnipuddy puts the truck into gear and the tires rub against the curb, I decide that if we're about to part forever, and if I'm his stranger just as he is mine, then it's my duty to exit his story with some style so that when he thinks about it from time to time, it won't be only bad memories. I set down my drink, run up to the truck, and motion for him to roll down the window.

"This dump is only a stopping point for a guy like you," I tell him.

"If you say so," Gunnipuddy says.

I step closer to the van, practically stick my head in the window, and lower my voice. "It was a good kiss, if you were wondering. I'm talking first rate."

Gunnipuddy can't help smiling a little at that.

"But John and I are planning to get married. Understand? That's why it could never work between us."

He glances at John and nods. "Okay."

I step away from the van, and he rolls up the window and drives away.

Does he find my words heartening? Comforting? Who the hell knows? But they are two truths and a lie, and they feel like the parting words of an important stranger. Words that a guy like Gunnipuddy, facing the odds, needs to hear.

What's Left of Musical Giants

After a month of sitting in his sunken den, listening to the great composers on thirty-threes and watching the fish tank, where the catfish munched the scuz and the prettier fish ate one another or leaped stupidly into the bubbling filter, Gene Barotta took a job at the mall. At the old mall. The new mall, just three miles farther down the road, had opened a year earlier. It had a multiplex and a food court. It was in a safer part of town, and its parking lot was brighter and better patrolled. This time of year, the new mall stayed open till eleven p.m. and had a North Pole exhibit. With the new mall so close by, there wasn't much reason to shop at the old mall. Unless you wanted to avoid the crowds. Or if you wanted to buy an electric organ for your home. Only the old mall sold home organs, at Richie's Famous Organ Store.

Gene would punch in an hour or so after his shift had started at the organ store and head immediately for black coffee and a currant scone at Bagels Plus. The teenage girls behind the counter wore tight aprons that accentuated their young curves. One girl in particular—eighteen maybe, with a splash of freckles on her nose—permitted Gene his joke, repeated daily. (Girl: *Is your scone stale?* Gene: *No—it's currant!*)

After lunch Gene would put in four or five hours on the Soundfast Genus model at the front of the organ store, playing and replaying "Silent Night" and "Sleigh Ride" and a jazzy version of "Feliz Navidad." The organ out front was like a fishing lure that hooked unsuspecting holiday shoppers. Retired couples, mostly. And foreigners. The mall-walkers would stop walking for a moment and nod their heads or tap their feet or maybe say how festive the music sounded, and Gene would force a smile, stop playing, and say to the woman, *I can teach you to play "Jingle Bells" inside of five minutes.* He would then guide the customers, who suspected they might be customers but weren't sure of it, into the store, where Gene would instruct the woman—always the woman—to play "Jingle Bells" with nothing but her two index fingers, accompanied by the organ's frantic Bossa Nova beat. Once she'd played it through, Gene would look at her and say, *You have a real knack for music, did you know that?*

Richie, the boss, would wander over and explain that the Soundfast Organ Company's sounds have been digitally sampled from the world's finest musicians. *We've got Benny Goodman's exact clarinet sound in there,* he'd say. Or, *That's Louis Armstrong's trumpet you're hearing.* Sometimes it was Louis Armstrong, other times Dizzy Gillespie or Roy Eldridge. Always one of the Big Band greats. Always a dead musician. *That's right, folks,* Riche would say, *we've got what's left of a dozen musical giants in every organ.* He would shepherd the customers into his office, shut the door, and hand them a finance application as if it were a Christmas present.

Gene always left Richie's Famous Organ Store at least an hour before closing, before the organs needed to be dusted and the carpet vacuumed. He'd taught music at the public high school in Breakneck Beach since 1962, when most of the county was nothing but woods and farmland. He'd taught through two wars, three if you counted Desert Storm. Through enough Presidents to fill up a room. So nobody was going to tell Gene Barotta to vacuum. To dust. To take the trash out to the dumpster. When Sammy and Ted, the other employees, complained, Richie said that when they owned a store, they could hire and fire whoever they damn well pleased. Gene was a keeper. Besides Richie, Gene was the only musician in the place. He inspired trust in the customers. He had knowledge, Richie explained, coming out of his ass.

During his interview, Gene had learned that Richie's Famous Organ Store was a contraction, not a possessive. Richie, not the organ store, was famous. Richie had once played electric guitar with a group called the Velvets. They'd had a hit in the sixties called "Ten-Four, Good Baby." Now, when no customers were in the store, Richie would call Gene into his office, close the door, and reminisce about the blinding heat of the stage lights, the hordes of fans chanting your name, the wild and insatiable groupies. Gene would nod in agreement, that, yes, life on the road was hard but the rewards were sweet. As if Gene had ever played in a band. As if he had ever traveled, other than once to Erie, Pennsylvania when his ex-wife had been ill, and then a second time for her funeral.

All those chicks screaming, Richie would say. *Like for the Beatles on Ed Sullivan. All that trim.*

Gene was to retire from the high school at the end of the school year. A dinner was to be held in his honor. A week before the school year started, however, the school's new principal had announced to Gene that the orchestra needed to become more equitable. Nothing wrong with high standards, he had explained. But this wasn't the New York Philharmonic, after all. Nobody was looking for their children to become the next Mozart. Do you see?

The principal enunciated each word as if Gene were senile or hard-of-hearing.

And so it had been decided, he went on to say, that no

longer would there be auditions for first-chair and second-chair. Instead, all students would rotate into first-chair. It would be fair. Everybody would have the experience of playing the lead role. The school board fully supported this idea. It made sense, when you thought about it.

"What about the football team?" Gene had asked. "Will all the football players get to be quarterback?"

The principal laughed as if Gene had told him a joke. They were in his office, and he tossed the pencil he'd been fidgeting with into a mug that said *World's Greatest Dad*. He leaned back in his chair. "Everybody understands the competitive nature of football. But music is an art, is it not?"

Gene agreed that it was.

"And isn't art," said the principal, raising a finger in the air, "above competition? Isn't art *better* than that?"

"Now look," Gene said, "what you're suggesting is damn stupid. And I won't do it." Gene suspected that his new principal went through entire days without ever listening to music. His car radio was tuned to the news. At home, he unwound to SportsCenter.

"Actually," said the principal, sitting forward again in his chair, "you will."

The day before school began, Gene selected the program for the fall concert. Schostakowitsch, *Symphony No. 10 in E Minor*. And Stravinsky, *The Rite of Spring*. Russian composers for the new principal who behaved like Stalin. Each piece infinitely beyond the orchestra's ability. And to make matters worse, Gene assigned the worst musicians to first chair. The freshman with the sprained thumb he made concertmaster. Anybody who squeaked and squawked, who honked and cracked, was guaranteed a soloist's spot. Three weeks before the concert, Gene mailed personal invitations to the principal, the vice principal, the board of education. In the hours before the concert he snuck around the rehearsal room, cutting slits into clarinet and oboe reeds with a pocket knife, removing the tympani heads and dropping in pennies that would rattle when the drum was struck.

Gene knew he wouldn't get fired. He had tenure. He was a year from retirement. And so he could afford to teach this valuable lesson to the new principal, to the board of education, the whole community. He had been commanded to make his orchestra more equitable. More fair. As if music had anything to do with fairness. Rachmaninov should have had one of his hands sliced off: with both, he played too well! The brilliant Mozart should have been lobotomized to stop him from writing an unfair number of beautiful operas. What people like the new principal didn't understand was that by making the orchestra "equitable," you dishonored the music. No— you spat on it. But they would learn.

During the performance, Gene changed all of the tempos from as rehearsed and intentionally cued solos at the wrong time. He cringed his way through the program, caught between hysterical laughing and sobbing as the students struggled valiantly and the orchestra chugged on, constantly on the verge of derailing.

Gene was grateful at least to be standing on his podium, facing the orchestra rather than the audience—because what must they be thinking? Was anybody still in attendance, or had everyone slipped out during the cacophonous *fortissimo* sections? And yet, when he slashed the baton through the air at the end of the Schostakowitsch, the applause began tentatively but became hearty. There were whistles. An hour later, when *The Rite of Spring* ground to a final, fumbling halt, people actually yelled "Bravo." At the reception afterwards in the school's cafeteria, parents praised Gene for having selected such a challenging program. For putting his students to the test. Gene shook hands with beaming board members. The principal brought him a plastic cup of root beer, clasped him on the shoulder, and said, "You're a team player, Gene, and I won't forget it." Then he added, "Bravo, Maestro," and clapped silently.

Gene downed the root beer in a single gulp and dropped the cup into the trash. Then he walked up to a pretty and talented flutist who was standing with a number of friends and their parents, and asked if he could squeeze her tits.

The next day he was home watching the fish tank. And the next. A month later, he was still trying to figure out why he'd done it, so close to that dinner in his honor.

He hadn't cared at all about the girl, or her tits. She was a good flutist but not a great one. She was forgettable. Once every five or six years, though, a student would play a string of notes so sweetly that Gene's spine tingled and his toes went numb. Didn't matter whether that student went on to work in a hardware store or a bowling alley or maybe a pharmacy. Didn't matter if the student ever played another note. Gene remembered these students not for their names or faces, or for anything they might have said, but for the notes played on a particular day, notes that the students themselves would never realize were any different in timbre or feeling from those of the day before or the day after.

And once every twelve or fifteen years, the entire orchestra, despite their youth, their artlessness, would nonetheless coalesce for four or eight bars of music, maybe only ten or fifteen seconds, but long enough to remind Gene not to deny the existence of God.

He'd had one year left. Eight months, actually. His career had spanned four decades. There was nothing more to prove. He could have said, Yes, sir, and done what the new principal had asked. But to do as asked meant to deny even the possibility for one last divine moment.

Richie paid his employees nine dollars an hour plus commission, though commissions were more theoretical than actual. In order to earn commissions you had to sell organs. The organ business might have thrived at one time, but the instrument had become a time capsule. Every built-in accompaniment sounded like a Depression-era combo. The Soundfast Organ Company catered to those willing to spend three or four thousand dollars in order to bring tranquility and amusement to their homes with *E-Z Play* versions of "Moonlight Serenade" or "String of Pearls."

Or ten thousand. Or twenty. All the way up to the Heritage model, a cherry wood monstrosity that'd take up an entire wall of your average-sized living room, retailing for thirty-six thousand dollars. Then again, the Heritage wasn't made for the average-sized living room. Sitting at the instrument, with its rows of controls and lights blinking on and off, seemed to Gene like being in the cockpit of a 747. Richie displayed the Heritage on a custom-built platform, kept it polished and dusted, and never let a customer anywhere near it. Not unless you'd already dropped ten grand on a Festival, or maybe sixteen on a Cotillion, having proven yourself susceptible to the charm of Richie's anachronistic and overpriced line of products.

At Richie's Famous Organ Store, the sales pitch was simple: teach the woman to play "Jingle Bells" with her two index fingers, and promise eight additional in-store lessons with any purchase. Part of Gene's job as Keyboard Associate was to teach these lessons, during which he was to introduce his students to the added features found in only the more expensive models. *Why don't you sit at the Cotillion today*, Gene would say. *It has automatic three-voice harmony.* Here, Richie felt, was where Gene's experience as a music teacher would pay off most: customer confidence. Gene earned a bonus of fifty dollars each time a student traded up. Fifty dollars that he could use. His job at Richie's Famous Organ Store wasn't just to get himself away from the gloom of his fish tank. When you ask to squeeze a sophomore's tits, you jeopardize your retirement income.

One day, after Richie had told Gene a vivid tale of yearning and triumph while traveling from Poughkeepsie to Binghamton in the Velvet's touring van, Gene explained to Richie why he'd gotten fired from Breakneck Beach High. Gene didn't try to explain the anger and frustration that had led to his lewd act. He didn't particularly want Richie's sympathy, or even his understanding. It was just that, after several weeks, Richie had been doing all of the talking. Gene felt as if he needed to keep up his end of the conversation.

Richie began laughing so hard that tears came to his eyes. "My, my," he said, and ran a hand through his graying hair. "Well, you've got a home here, my perverted friend."

Gene looked out through the glass door of Richie's office and into the store. Sammy, maybe a year or two out of high school, sat on the rug, hunched over one of the automobile magazines he always carried with him, one hand flipping pages, the other pulling greasy French fries out of a paper sack. At the front of the store, Ted, whose tie was a clip-on, who had a sore on his bottom lip that seemed never to heal, banged out some unrecognizable melody on the Soundfast Genus, while the mall-strollers, who were few in number, paid no attention.

"I'm not so sure the organ business has such a hot future," Gene said.

Richie looked out into the store, but the same raw data evidently brought a different conclusion. "Oh, it's just the music business," he said. "It's cyclical."

"But it's December twenty-first and the mall's dead," Gene said. "Isn't there supposed to be a Christmas rush?"

Richie stood, opened the door to his office and called out, "Hey, Teddy, you gonna sell some organs today?"

Ted stopped playing and trotted to the back of the store. "What?"

"I said, are you going to sell some organs today?"

"*Fuck*, yeah." He gave Richie a stern look, as if Richie had questioned something basic and certain—whether he intended ever to bathe again, or to call his mother. "*Fuck*, yeah, Richie." He jogged back to the front of the store and began his unrecognizable tune where, presumably, he had left off.

Richie swung the door closed. "All we got to do is keep the troops motivated."

Gene kept looking out into the nearly deserted mall. "Maybe you'd better focus on keeping the customers motivated."

"Trust me." Richie smacked Gene on the leg. "There's an ass for every bench."

Richie always told the staff to look busy whenever the young Puerto Rican couples came by. He claimed that the Puerto Ricans would admire the organs, take up all your time, but would never buy a damn thing other than sheet music. One day, two of them walked right up to Sammy, who was trolling for customers outside the store, playing "White Christmas." Ordinarily Sammy, Ted, and Gene would rotate to the front of the store every fifteen minutes or so, but Ted had called in sick, and Gene wasn't in the mood. So Sammy had been out there for over an hour playing the same song. The man had his arm around his lady. She had shiny black hair and a mole on her cheek, and Gene found her exceptionally beautiful. This couple often walked the mall together, but as far as Gene knew had never stopped to listen. Now they stood next to Sammy and the lady hummed along with the music, glancing up at her man as if for approval. Sammy hadn't played a single note before starting work here a year earlier, and a butterfly beating its wings in Timbuktu was enough to throw him off. This beautiful woman standing so close was quite a distraction. He lost the beat immediately, then the melody, then the chords. Sammy was a nervous kid, the sort who wakes up one morning after high school graduation to find he's all alone, that everyone he's ever known has joined the army or enrolled in community college. He had a habit of blinking his eyes too often.

He stopped playing and just stood there, watching the keys, blinking like mad. He took a deep breath, switched beats from Soft Swing to Big Band, and began playing "New York, New York," which Richie didn't like because it wasn't seasonal. But Sammy's repertoire was limited.

"Well?" the man asked. He waited while Sammy hunted for the melody with his stiff fingers. "Does Liberace want to earn a commission today or not?"

Sammy stopped playing. "You interested in this Genus? It's on sale for just under two thou." He'd gotten so flustered that he'd forgotten all about the lesson you were supposed to give the lady.

"Nah—we want something bigger than that. Something nice." The man pointed to the back of the store. To the Heritage. "How much is that one?"

"That one? You want that one?" Sammy yelled into the store: "Richie!"

While Sammy had been playing, Gene had been sitting at an organ in the middle of the store, paging through Sammy's auto magazines. Gene hadn't read an auto magazine for decades and was struck by all the women who were nearly naked. It would be worth buying this magazine just for the women.

Sammy was interested in the cars. He rode the bus to the mall each day and had dreams of buying a used Camaro. And so when Gene looked up from the magazine and told Sammy that their boss wasn't around, that he'd gone for a sandwich, Sammy's eyes lit up. Probably he saw giant dollar signs. Richie would have insisted on steering this Puerto

Rican couple to the low-end Genus, if he didn't kick them out of the store altogether. After they bought their sheet music—or, more likely, nothing—he would huddle with Gene and Sammy and say, "Don't let 'em waste your time. They don't have jobs, so they'll waste your whole day if you let 'em."

Still. What if they were the one-in-a-million customer? What if they were rich?

"Gene," Sammy said, leading the couple toward the rear of the store, "Why don't you show these nice folks how the Heritage sounds."

As Gene was about to close the auto magazine, his gaze caught a particular advertisement. No bikini models in this one. Just a family standing in the driveway in front of their Volvo. The daughter, for no reason that Gene could tell, held a flute in her hands, poised to play. An asinine ad, for why on earth would she be playing the flute in her driveway? Still, her pale face, her slightly bewildered expression reminded Gene of the flutist, *his* flutist, the sophomore. Which reminded him that today was the Friday night before Christmas, which meant that tonight was Breakneck Beach High's holiday concert.

Gene left the magazine on the nearest bench and went over to the Heritage. He sat down and searched the console for the waltz rhythm. There were three. He chose the Viennese Waltz, pressed the volume pedal to the floor, and began a sweeping version of "Voices of Spring,"— *"Frühlingsstimmen"*—by the great Johann Strauss II. Suddenly the store sounded like a carousel gone mad, as music from the Heritage burst forth from its twelve speakers, causing the mall walkers to stop in their tracks and employees from the shoe store across the way to crane their necks. The Heritage, Gene had to admit, sounded better than the other models, though it, too, was but a caricature of an actual orchestra. All the same, he felt powerful triggering, with a single key, the sound of thirty violins in perfect unison. Thirty violins supported by a dozen cellos in the warm lower octave; the accompaniment added French horns, trumpets, tympani...an entire symphony with two fingers, or as Gene used, all ten, making the music sound grand and majestic and vibrant, a perfect orchestra where nobody ever cracked a note or missed a cue, where you had total control, where a swell in volume from *pianissimo* to *fortissimo* was as simple as pressing the gas pedal of your car.

When Gene stopped playing, he was breathless. Had he played for only a minute? Or five, or ten? The small group that had gathered outside the store looked at one another as if waking up after a long flight, then dispersed. The woman in the store had unlocked herself from the man's grip sometime during Gene's performance and now stood so close to Gene that strands of her hair lay on his shoulder. He could smell the sweat underneath her perfume. "I'll bet," Gene said, looking up at her, "that I can get you playing this instrument inside of five minutes."

She let out a deep breath. "I'll bet you can."

He couldn't. This woman was undoubtedly the most tone-deaf, rhythmically deficient woman who ever lived. She sat beside him at the Heritage, and he placed her smooth fingers with their manicured nails on the keyboard. He played on the lower octave, she on the upper. It was fucking "Jingle Bells," but in the end, "Jingle Bells" bested her. All he could do was teach her "Chopsticks," the instrument set to Vibraphone ("Lionel Hampton's exact sound!"), and accompanied by a slow Romantic Waltz rhythm that she couldn't even keep pace with. She would play the wrong notes and the man would lay a hand on her neck and offer encouraging words. That was his job, maybe, to believe in his wife's potential. But Gene had taught music for forty-five years and had developed a laser-like eye for potential.

This woman had none. A year from now, she would still be playing "Chopsticks." For her, the Heritage would never be more than a thirty-six-thousand-dollar "Chopsticks" machine. And knowing this about her made Gene want desperately to sell this organ to her. He wanted this couple, who were obviously in love, to throw away thousands of dollars. The winter concert was tonight, and rather than at school where he belonged, Gene was here, hocking organs in the old mall, in a store that smelled like burned grease and cheap furniture polish. After a month of working at Richie's Famous Organ Store, Gene still felt superior to the job, superior to Richie and Sammy and Ted and all the people who had ever worked or shopped here. But he didn't want to feel superior anymore. He wanted to feel sleazy. To belong.

When the woman finally played "Chopsticks" correctly, Gene shut off the power before she could try again. "So now that you're a pro," he said, forcing the smile he wore whenever, after a concert, he had to meet the parents of his less capable students, "can't you picture this instrument in your living room?"

Nobody ever just walked in off the street and bought the Heritage. It cost too much. And yet there the couple sat in Richie's office, filling out a finance application. Sammy hovered in the doorway while Gene completed the transaction. He would fax the application to the finance company and, within the hour, receive a reply. The man and woman—Julio and Raquel Rivera—decided to roam the mall while the finance company made up their mind.

"I can't believe we're doing this!" Raquel Rivera's eyes were wide with excitement.

"Me either, baby." Julio was smiling, dazed.

"Congratulations," Sammy said to the couple, shook their hands firmly—as he was taught to do after a purchase—and guided them out of the store.

The moment they were gone, Gene gripped Sammy's arm hard enough to erase the grin from his face. "This deal goes through, I get half the commission. Understood?"

Sammy looked frightened for a moment, but then his grin returned. "Don't worry, Grandpa, you'll get your money." He rubbed the top of Gene's head and trotted to the front of the store. He began playing "White Christmas" again, the organ louder than before, the tempo faster. Today was his lucky day, he must have figured—maybe he could sell *two* Heritages.

Gene left the store and walked through the mall to the Pharmacy Depot to buy cigarettes, keeping a lookout for Raquel and Julio. He didn't want to jinx the deal, talking to them before it was final. He bought his cigarettes and went outside to smoke, where it was cold and would likely get him sick. The sky must have been orange and pink thirty minutes earlier, but all that was left now were the dregs of sunset, a sooty gray that each minute became blacker. The school concert would begin soon, but even though for four decades he had spent five days a week there, ten months each year, he couldn't imagine walking into that building ever again. The walls would look strange and institutional. The air would smell familiar, but wrong.

The area in front of the mall was like a wind tunnel, and Gene wrapped his arms around himself. He wore a sports coat and tie but should have worn his overcoat. Nearby, other mall employees smoked, too, waiting for the next bus, hunching their shoulders in the cold. The lot wasn't empty, but neither was it full. And yet Christmas was in four days. People should be fighting one another for parking spots. Drivers should be cursing pedestrians. Pedestrians should be cursing the high prices. The foul weather. The entire fucking holiday season. But none of this was going on. Clearly, the old mall was doomed. Gene tossed the cigarette butt on the ground and went back inside. He stopped at Bagels Plus for coffee and to flirt with his favorite.

"Where's the other one?" he asked. "The pretty one?"

The woman behind the counter wiped her hands on her apron and pursed her lips. "Sara's on break."

"Oh, hell," Gene said. "Just forget it, then."

When he returned to the store, Richie was in his office, leaning back in his chair, holding the Riveras' finance application. "So there *is* a sucker born every minute." With a flourish, he handed the paperwork to Gene. "Julio and Raquel Rivera? You'll never see them again. Listen to me when I tell you, my friend, they've got nothing better to do than waste your time." Gene glanced down at the application, which had been denied. "And where the hell's Sammy? I came back to an empty store."

As Gene was saying he had no idea where Sammy had gone, muffled sounds came from the closet. "The hell?" Gene followed Richie to the supply closet. Richie swung open the door.

"Whoa!" he said, and took a step back. "Whoa, whoa— what's going on here?"

Sammy yanked his hands out from underneath the girl's white t-shirt. They were both on their knees. When she spun her head toward them, Gene didn't recognize her at first without her Bagels Plus cap or apron, and with her flushed face masking the freckles. Gene was wrong about her being eighteen. She wasn't even close. She was just a kid making out with Sammy in a closet.

Sara forced a smile. "Hi."

"Oh, no. Not here you don't," Richie said. "You take that business someplace else."

"Sorry, Richie," Sammy stammered, blinking wildly. "We—"

"You two get out of here. Clean yourselves up. Go on." He waited while Sammy and Sara stood and left the closet.

"That's right, you two get out of here. Sammy, take an hour and decide if you still want this job. And *you*"—he pointed at the girl, who was looking down at the carpet—"just be glad I'm not your father."

The two of them left the store quickly. Richie returned to his office, trailed by Gene, and flopped down on his chair, which wheezed under the weight.

"He was celebrating his big commission check," Gene said.

"Holy smokes," Richie said, shaking his head. "What kind of business does he think I'm running here? Who does he think I am?"

After Sammy returned to hear that the Riveras' loan had been denied, he seemed lifeless, sitting in a corner, arms around his knees, looking at his magazine but not turning any pages, until he clocked out and left at eight o'clock without even a goodbye. Richie paced in front of the store for a while, muttering to himself about how goddamn beat he was, until Gene offered to stay and close the store.

"You mean it?" Richie said, but then must have thought better than to wait for Gene to change his mind. "Adiós, then." He collected the trash from underneath his desk, slung the plastic bag over his shoulder, and left the store.

Alone, Gene went into Richie's office and shut the door. Sat in Richie's chair. The holiday concert was underway. Gene remembered his first holiday concert at Breakneck Beach High. He had been hired to start up a marching band. But when football season wound down, he'd persuaded the principal to let him start up a school orchestra.

The orchestra, if you could call it that, had thirteen students. Too many flutes. No low brass. No percussion. They'd rehearsed after school twice a week in the chemistry lab. There had been no money to buy musical scores, and his orchestra's instrumentation was so peculiar anyway that for weeks Gene would sit each night at his kitchen table, scoring arrangements. Their first concert had lasted twenty-five minutes. It hadn't gone well. But Gene had himself an orchestra.

Just before the mall closed at nine-thirty, there were three soft taps on the office door. Gene looked up and saw that the Riveras had returned—about four hours late. When Gene opened the door, Raquel and Julio started speaking very quickly.

Raquel said, "We had to come back...we feel terrible..."

Julio said, "We knew that our loan would never get approved..."

"But we didn't have the heart to say no..."

"We're in a lot of debt. You can't imagine the problems we've had..."

Gene sat and listened. They had to get this off their chests. He picked up a pencil and twirled it in his fingers.

"We wanted to apologize for taking your time..."

Gene waited until they were done. He put the pencil down, looked up at them, and smiled. "But you've been *approved*," he said. He hadn't planned on saying that. But now it was out there.

Julio scrunched up his face. "Really?"

"The fax came through hours ago—the whole amount, approved. I can have the instrument delivered, let's see..." As he spoke, he looked on the list by the phone for the delivery company's number. "...on Monday, most likely. Definitely by Tuesday. In time for Christmas." He picked up the receiver and dialed a series of numbers that connected him to nobody, and the couple stood there looking at Gene while he pretended to leave a message with all the particulars: the model number, the Riveras' home address, the promise he'd made to his customers that they'd have the instrument before Christmas.

He hung up the phone. "Just think how happy your

holidays will be this year," he said, a last bit of salesmanship, "knowing you can have a sing-along whenever you want." As if the Riveras were thinking about sing-alongs. No, their faces were hardening with the realization of this new financial burden. The monstrosity they believed they'd just bought and would have to find a place for in their home. The instrument that neither of them, they both now realized with absolute certainty, would ever touch. Their thoughts were not on sing-alongs, but rather on their debt, and their shame, and their anger at this tricky salesman who'd recognized in them the flaw of pride; that their pride would keep them from backing out of their purchase now that the financing had been approved and the delivery arranged. "Thank you," they said to Gene, but they said it the way you say it to a doctor after a painful exam. They said thank you, but what they really meant was, *How could you?*

After they left the store, the lights in the mall dimmed. The mall was closing. In other stores, employees were vacuuming rugs and dusting merchandise. Gene lit a cigarette, and when it was gone he wrote a note to Richie in sloppy script that he wouldn't be back anymore. He left the note on the desk, then shut off the store's lights, locked up, lit another cigarette, and went outside, where the parking lot was dark and desolate. He never stayed this late, and to soothe his fears as he headed to his car he found himself singing "Moonlight Serenade."

Gene wasn't a singer but could carry a tune. He sang slowly, listening with curiosity to his own raspy timbre. Then he stopped singing because he sounded—crooning in the parking lot—like a crazy old man. There was one line left to the verse, but he felt foolish and didn't sing it.

The car was still a ways away. Maybe a gang of kids would slide out of the dark and attack him. Bash him from behind with a bat, or a pipe, steal his wallet, and nobody would find him until the mall opened in the morning. Or he could get shot in the gut. Or cut with a razor. Or even if he wasn't attacked, his heart could begin lurching wildly anyway, or stop beating altogether. He could have a thrombotic stroke, like his own father. There were any number of ways to die between here and the car. It was the sort of thing you thought about at this time of night, at this time of year, at this point in your life. A walk to the car became a test.

But if Gene passed the test, if none of those things happened, then before he went home tonight he would drive the three extra miles to the new mall, probably circle it once or twice, watching the crowds, dazed from shopping, returning to their cars—balancing packages and digging for keys—and then he would park his own car and go inside, in search of a job among the living.

MICHAEL KARDOS co-directs the creative writing program at Mississippi State University. His short stories were cited as Notable Stories in the 2009 and 2010 editions of *Best American Short Stories* and have appeared in *The Southern Review, Crazyhorse, Prairie Schooner, Pleiades, Blackbird,* and many other magazines and anthologies. Kardos grew up on the Jersey Shore, received a degree in music from Princeton University, and for the next decade played the drums in a number of bands, including Thunder Road, "The Ultimate Tribute to Springsteen." He has an M.F.A. in fiction from The Ohio State University and a Ph.D. from the University of Missouri. More information can be found at www.michaelkardos.com.

Cover artist **MEGAN SNIDER** is a writer, editor, cupcake baker and photographer from Waldorf, Maryland. Since receiving her first point-and-shoot camera after college graduation, she's been actively taking photos of life in suburban Washington, D.C., and her travels, family and dinner. Snider is a columnist for three D.C.-area newspapers and blogs about reading, travel, food and love at www.writemeg.com.

Acknowledgments

Thanks to Michelle Herman for her wisdom and tireless encouragement, and to Christopher Coake and Michael Piafsky for reading and rereading nearly everything I've ever written. I also want to thank Brian Barker, Erica Beeney, Nicky Beer, William Bradley, Jeff Butler, Keith Cooper, Teline Guerra, Scott Kaukonen, Lauren Kenney, Stephanie Lauer, Kelly Magee, Nathan Oates, Alis Sandosharaj, Tony Varallo, Nick White, and Amy Wilkinson. I was lucky to attend graduate programs at The Ohio State University and the University of Missouri, where many of these stories were written; I want to thank my inspiring and generous professors Lee K. Abbott, Trudy Lewis, Lee Martin, Erin McGraw, Speer Morgan, and Marly Swick. Thanks to Mark Winegardner, Alice McDermott, and the Sewanee Writers' Conference, as well as Ayun Halliday and the Santa Fe Writers Project. Thanks to the editors and judges who championed these stories before the book had a home, including Pinckney Benedict, Laura Benedict, Laurie Champion, Roland Goity, John Gould, Michael Griffith, Ben Hart, Jesse Lee Kercheval, Jeanne Leiby, Brett Lott, Hilda Raz, and Jeff Stautz. And my deepest thanks to Kevin Morgan Watson and Press 53 for giving it a home, and such a fine, welcoming one at that. Thanks, too, to my supportive and kind colleagues at Mississippi State University, and especially to Becky Hagenston and Richard Lyons, writers I admire and who happen to work right down the hall. I'd also like to thank Josh Kutchai, consummate artist, as well as my unfailingly, delightfully, even aggressively supportive family. Finally, I want to thank Catherine Pierce in letters so large that this book cannot contain them.

MK

Breinigsville, PA USA
16 February 2011
255684BV00001B/164/P